The Muse in

Annoying

The Machines had be
months. One was one of the c
automatic Printing Machines. It could be left to run till it ran out of feed stock; or set to stop after a number of pages have been printed and was all mechanical in nature. It was one of the only two machines that were still in the old Print Room in the Basement. The other; with more features; was the huge Bremman & Költz; large format Roll fed “Lithographic” machine with optional cutting system. It had been modified with the later addition of a “Transmutable” image bed for printing monochrome dot matrix images in a fairly high resolution. Or with the other additional beds could print colour the roll being threaded through them via ancillary rollers. It used to be just Stamp printed impact forms; for posters and newsprint; the electronic addition used old single industrial Thyristor arrays to control the position of the dots in the matrices when it was first upgraded. They too had been replaced at some point with more modern units; which were faster and more reliable. It was used these days to print exclusive wrapping papers for special orders from the Gift department in the main Ground floor of the Department Store above. The Smaller machine; The Monnan Brigand; would manage up to A1 at a push. But it tended to struggle to print more than twenty copies at a time in that size format. And they had to be fed back through the printer for each colour for colour prints changing the printing plate each time. It still located each pass through perfectly. It was used for short runs of reproduced numbered prints of works taken from a catalogue. Some older Customers preferred the look of the finished product of the Monnan over the same sized

reproductions of the Bremman & Költz. It had a slight shift displacement between passes for the different colours. The New electronic Epson Large format Lasers upstairs in the Offices out performed it in quality. But tended to baulk at long runs; sometimes running out of toners mid run without warning. A flaw in the Firmware; the fix for which the Store's IT maintenance was still "getting around to".

Charlie Watts was in charge of the Basement Print room and maintained the lovey old machines. Modern things were all plastics and cheap "tinny parts that broke at the slightest provocation". Or complicated electronics that cost a fortune to get replacements for. It was usually cheaper to just replace the whole machine. But his charges were built solidly. They had a "soul" to them. He had just completed a thorough overhaul of the Bremman and was going to do a test run that evening when the store shut for the night. He had some "Specialist" Images that he used for test prints and a relative had asked for some fresh copies when he did a check run. They would be on the cheapest stock to make sure the pressure sensing worked properly and the machine didn't tear the print. If it did them fine; it would do any stock... even eighth inch card. He was going to do the Monnan the weekend coming. That was a more intricate process and could take a whole day to dismantle the active parts and clean, oil and grease, and refit them. The Rollers and hand feeds on that machine were a detachable section that could be maintained separately. He had two "Spares" in standby, one ready to exchange in an emergency, one prepped to exchange when the third was taken off for maintenance. The springs on the assemblies needed fine adjustment to keep the registration spot on. He was probably one of only three people in the town that could maintain these devices in tip top order.

Tom Hardaker the Shops General Manager had been at Hamptons General for the same length of time as Charlie. They had both risen from the shop floor. Only Charlie's world had gone down as Tom's had gone up. Tom would be using the early retirement option and his replacement was in "learning the ropes". Oh the lad had all the "technical" knowledge, but the "Practical" skills could take years to perfect and master. Less time if you really put your mind to it. Charlie had an Apprentice too. The Company had the idea of "leasing" the machines to History Societies. So School kids could learn the "old" ways of how things were done. The reason for the maintenance was because of one of those "Educational Experiences" as the Upper Management were fond of calling them; and was due next month and some Artist had given a few of his lesser works to be "reproduced". In the case of the Monnan; that involved photo etching up to six plates per work of six colours of ink. Each had to be printed one over the other in a strict sequence. And the machine cleaned carefully between each run. That was similar with the Bremman; but the Cleaning was simpler and done with an automated flushing system. The Bremman used an Optical location system to register each over print, hence the slight offset that could occur in long runs. The Monnan a rigid physical lock system and never misaligned unless a spring or two weakened with age. But was slower than the Bremman. Hence it was used to print store specific Wrapping Papers for small gifts; at Christmas and other seasonal occasions. Also Promotional posters for Products on special offer etc.

Charlie's apprentice Derek Barnes, a Yorkshire boy, was eager to get started. And helped Charlie get ahead by going in and disengaging the sections he wanted to take out, dismantle; clean and reassemble. Derek would then refit and "lock down". They had done this now enough times to have it off to a fine art. Tom once did a stopwatch timing of the pair. Even some of the "Competition" teams were slower at times. It depended on whether it was a part or full maintenance. Tom's learner; Simon Boswell, was fascinated. He was a Steam Railway Enthusiast and loved the old machinery. He'd once seen an American Newspaper printing machine that was powered by a small single cylinder steam reciprocator engine; in Ohio when over on a holiday. Watching these two work was an education in itself. He could understand why the school kids found it fascinating just standing watching the machinery go through its paces.

"I wish more modern companies would learn from Hamptons General. Sometimes it paid to keep the "old" ways alive" Simon had said when The Top brass had paid one of their rare visits. They'd had a number of visits from various TV production Companies over the years. All of whom went away awe struck. Even Fred Dibnah when he was alive had made a courtesy call to the Rear Yard of the Shop in his Traction Engine. That had Simon enraptured. It had done the Stores reputation wonders. Charlie was asked one year to do some Harrod's Wrapping Papers for the Main Harrod's Store in London. Apparently a certain Royal Personage had heard about the old machines and wanted some "specials" running off. For a handsome reward of course. The prestige alone had seen a massive upsurge in sales that year. The two set about the Bremman with vigour and finished early enough to start the dismantling of the Monnan. Even though it was smaller, it was far more complicated. Springs; linkages, chains and belts (some individual lapped leather pieces) had to be removed in a particular sequence and replaced in the exact reverse order. Charlie had all the details firmly engraved in his mind. There were manuals covering the processes. And even Derek was getting good enough to only keep checking occasionally now. He was learning the machines secrets and whims every time he used them. He could; like Charlie tell if a part was wearing by the slight change in sound made by each of the actions. That was why Derek had ordered a new linkage kit for number two feed system. The Maker kept a pattern book for third party manufacturers to make and repair parts. Not even some Modern Car Manufacturers did that these days. It was down to enthusiasts to recreate the pattern.

That was why it came as no surprise that Simon and some of his Steam Buddies dropped by as the two were packing up for the day; they always expected one or two late visitors

"The Store is closing Sunday all day for a refurbishment of the Haberdashery Department. They want volunteers to help dismantle and shift the old Counter stock out tonight and over Saturday and early Sunday morning. Me and the lads will be in to help out. You and Derek interested. The Old Man said some of the Sales units are going up for grabs. You could do with some down here to put some of your tiny spares in I would imagine" Simon said. One of the others was eyeing the Bremman

"This is a beast; I worked as a reporter in a provincial paper when I was younger. They printed the whole broadsheet circulation on two of these. Got to the stage of including full colour spreads then the business was incorporated into some Conglomerate from Canada" He said. He introduced himself as Bernie Falstaff; originally from a remote Scottish highland community; now a resident in Dorset for his sins. He'd been a reporter nearly all his adult life. Till a leg injury in the field; reporting from Beirut, had him "retired on medical grounds". "There's still some pieces of shrapnel in there. I sometimes scare the Grandbairns by tapping them with a pen. The clinks make them cringe" he said chuckling. Charlie liked this fellow

"Simon; that might be worth a looksee. I suppose they will be giving the stuff they don't want to the Local Bonfire Committee for the Fireworks celebrations" he said

"Actually no. One of the local Kids schools is getting some for their woodwork room. They've been getting one of those CAD driven Routing tables with automatic bit changing. It has hundreds of different bits so they need something with plenty of drawers. You could probably use three down here with all the bits you have to keep" Simon answered. They all left the Basement together. Two of the Cooks from the restaurant were just leaving having put together the sandwich order for "elevenses" for the volunteers. Coming in late tonight and Saturday after store closing to start taking the wall units down.

"Evening Charlie... Derek... Our Maisie wants your young lad here to take a look at her bike sometime. It keeps snapping chains. It's costing a fortune getting them done at Mike's Cycles" Charlene said

“I’ll be free Tuesday night after my college work. Mrs Figgie” he replied

“Anyone fancy a pint before they go for evening meals?” Simon asked

“Need you ask” the other enthusiasts said. Charlie declined, but Derek said he’d join them. Besides Charlie’s missus was waiting for him. If he didn’t scoot she’d be giving him the silent treatment all night.

In the silence of the darkened Basement. Faint noises could be heard as some of the ceiling boards settled back down after being vibrated out of place by the test run of the large Bremman. The take up unit for the paper feed was detached from the Monnan and partially disassembled with a careful note made of where they had got to on one work order log. And a work order log for the reassembly sequence started. The quiet was disconcerting in that darkness. The only odd periodic sound was the pulse of the Clock mechanism... At first that is. The Store has a system of Clocks in all the departments that took a pulse to operate the minute hand and gearing to do the rest of the clock function. The Master Clock was in the Accounts office and was a brutal looking Art deco chrome pillar with a severe looking face with bars instead of numerals. All the other clocks got their pulse from its relays inside that pillar. That circuitry was arranged as sort of ring circuits for each floor, five in all and six independent feeds to the Basement, the Goods Inwards and the Mail/dispatch room where some packaging was also done. Two clocks in each department. These clocks had time card punches. For the staff to clock in and out of their respective departments. Colour coded punch cards denoting each department and had the workers details on them. These were collected weekly on a Tuesday for the Wages section of Accounts to process. Everybody being paid a week in arrears.

A tiny scraping sound could be heard coming from near to the Monnan... And a faint pale blue glow and a moving, a tiny shadow went along with the scraping. Something with tiny; minute hands was doing intensive work. Something was doing the work Charlie and Derek had left until tomorrow; Saturday. Whatever it was worked methodically and persistently. It was putting back together its home. Repairing tiny imperfections with even tinier tools. When it was satisfied it went into the Machine and slid shut the metal cover over the fuse box unit. It was now around three in the morning and where there had been a dismantled press feed unit... there now stood a complete machine. It had been repaired, reworked and refitted so precisely it was as if it hadn't been taken off in the first place. The work orders had also been completed in a spidery hand.

Charlie made it in time and he didn't get the cold shoulder. Leona his wife joked he'd get that in his sandwiches in his Bait box tomorrow. She meant it too; their married son had got two huge shoulders of ham given so he saved one for them. It had taken a while to cook. But the meat just fell from the bone. They had an early supper as Charlie wanted to get an early start on the Monnan. Try and get as much done during the early trade times. He told her about the refurbishment

"Ooh; I wonder if they're throwing out those old Tailors dummies they used to use in the display for the work Clothes?" she mused

"I can ask. They's closing half day to get an early start

some were starting this evening. There were some in prepping the wall units; to be dismantled tomorrow, yesterday night. I heard one of the Backroom boys cussing because the driver slipped; the bolt heads were that tight. Charlene reckons they finished just before we did then; as we did tonight. Oh I tell you what. There were two mahogany counter units, the small ones with the cupboards out front and the drawers out back. They'd be ideal for our Sadie and her man. Match their furniture a treat and they aint plywood either" he said. She liked that idea; and said Robby would get them in the van if he could get dibs on 'em

"I wouldn't mind one of the bottom under counter units to go in my Needlework room. Our Sadie's old room. It would tidy up all those boxes I'm using now. And you could have them for your Garage. You're always going on about lack of boxes for bits" she said. He would talk with Tom in the morning. They'd both been there long enough to be able to put their mark on an item afore others. Except old Jeremy in Accounts. He must be nearly sixty seven, but "won't retire till he gets that bad with his joints he can't walk" he kept saying. He would too; he was stubborn old coot.

The alarm woke him. He was in the spare room so as not to disturb Leona. She'd had a couple of Brandy wines and with her Steroid meds; she slept soundly. Sadie would call in to check on her soon he thought. Their daughter was the district Nurse now; Leona made her keep her key "Just in case".

He washed; shaved and dressed and picked up his lunch bag. Leona had made more than enough sandwiches for three let alone one. And there was a bottle of Mackie's as well. He'd give that to Jeremy; he could do with it more;

Charlie and Derek would have Coffee, Derek always brought an extra flask. Why Jeremy was in on Saturdays, he'd found out unexpectedly once. It was unusual seeing as when the weekend accounts were not ever done till a Monday morning; and was odd. But Charlie had found out one Saturday. He'd found him in the Home Entertainments Department. The Old Coot was playing his Jazz records in one of the booths. Harriet hated the Music Style so he resorted to getting his Fix by colluding with the young girl behind the Record counter. Jeremy had a good taste in the music genre. Only the best artists and the best recordings for him. This morning the weather service had hit the nail on the head. It had been a clear night and there was a thick morning frost. The basement skylights were covered in a white fur. Derek was at the Doors to the Loading lift scratching his head

"You're not going to believe what is down there. And someone has blocked our stairwell with boxes again. Brace yourself; I couldn't believe what I saw when I opened up after fighting through the piles. They must be for all the loose items from the refurb. We'll use the lift" He said and Charlie joined him already bewildered. As the lift descended he realised immediately that the area they'd left the parts to dismantle was bare... And the Monnan was intact!?

"How? What? Who?" He said in quick succession. The Press gleamed as if it was new; both of them did. Whoever had put the things back together had polished the brass, and cleaned the paint work to within an inch of its life. They gleamed.

"You tell me. I hadn't even started cleaning the Levers

and ratchets. And there's something else. That test run we were going to do has been done... and they are totally perfect, not a flaw on any of 'em" Derek said an odd look on his face... Tom was walking around the Basement measuring up

"You Lad's done an amazing job with these machines. I don't even remember them being this Spic and Span when I first started here. I had to come down to deliver Old Guthrie's mail every morning. I've set some units aside for you for down here. The lads had got more loose that we thought. The School; can have a few more for the Gym locker rooms. The Old Man just wants them gone" he said. Charlie and Derek told him how they'd left things last night

"Ask Simon; he was here with his Train Buddies" Derek said. Charlie asked about the units and the Tailors Dummies

"Sure; they were destined for the tip anyway. And you're right about those units too. I'll get one of the delivery lads to drop them off at your Sadie's save Robby a journey, they all go past their place anyway... We found something odd behind some of the units mind you. I don't know what the Upper lot will make of it... When you set this place for a short run of the posters that artist chap wants; come up to Haberdashery and take a gleg" Tom said mysteriously. Derek was looking at the work logs

"It's like that ruddy tale about the Cobbler and the fairies. I know how I left things last night. And... oh; now that's peculiar. What a weird looking handwriting" he said as he looked at the work logs. "Jeremy in accounts will like the meticulous costing of each part used" he said and handed the logs to Tom

"It's like a Spider has scrawled the words. They are so thin and fine. I feel like a one of those victims on a prank show. Well; setting the machines up will not take long, we may as well do it and have a coffee to steady our nerves eh?" he said. Charlie agreed. And Derek was right. The etched plates had come back from the metalworkers carefully wrapped and meticulously clean. They'd do the sequence on the Bremman first, that could be set and forgotten about. They'd set the Monnan to do the first colour and let it run through its quota while they went to find out what Tom was on about.

When they left the machines to do their runs; the two of them took the service elevator up to the floor where Haberdashery was being "gutted". Tom; Simon and Old Man Hagan the Senior Floor Manager, were stood in front of the wall that had been where the Box drawers and Shelving had been. The wall was one huge mural

"Wow! That's the Greek Muses that is" Derek said

"Oh! So you recognised it too" Hagan said "I've been trying to find out who commissioned it. And when. The company records were decimated when that incendiary crashed through the place during the War. I did find a reference to the artist Linel Delaine. He was a Dutch itinerant; from Amsterdam. Came over before the War and did commissions for a number of large department stores. Only there he used large canvases... This is on Gesso" he added

"Old Guthrie would have known more. He was here

during all of the bombings hereabouts" Charlie said "Pity he died two years ago. It is remarkably detailed. He must have used a single hair brush for some of those strokes in the Muses hair" Charlie added

"To be fair I just don't know what to do with it. That wall was going to have one of those huge video screen systems to display featured products and interactive ordering system customers could order goods through or for payment and delivery without having to wait in a cue. But this is too good to destroy. That Artist guy has contacted a Gallery expert in London he knows. The man was getting a flight this morning" Tom looked at his watch "He should be landing about now from Stanstead. He's only ever been this far north once before. When the Public Baths in York got that daft makeover. And they found all that Art Deco stuff under the panels of the walls in the "Directors lounge"" he added. Jeremy from accounts came in with two ledgers looking perplexed

"Someone has done half the work I was going to do Monday. And a good job of it too. Today's till receipts will be the last entries before the calculations Monday, but I don't recognise the hand... look" he said and handed Hagan the books. Derek caught a glimpse. He'd brought the Logs up to show Jeremy; it was the same spidery hand. He showed Jeremy the logs and the man's nervous twitch ticked in his face.

"Who the heck is this person?" he was close to breaking. Charlie gave him the Mackie's and settled him down

"You look like you need this more than I do. You should see the machines in the Basement" Charlie said

“Don’t tell me they’re broken beyond repair. I couldn’t take that after this.” Jeremy said

“Far from it. They look almost as good as new. Ask Tom he was down there this morning” Charlie said. Tom confirmed

“It’s the Pixies” a voice from behind them said. It was the Janitor Fred Braithwaite; “My predecessor said that during the thirties the place experienced a lot of strange goings on. I found all my equipment in my lockers tidied up when I came in this morning. All the windows in the Executive suite washed and polished so clean you could eat your dinner off them; if you had a mind to. And there’s something odd in the Packaging area too. Beryl says it’s so neat and tidy it’s like a show piece display” he added “Whenever anything like this happened before; the then Manager always used to blame it on the Pixies… well he *was* from Cornwall” Fred said

“Funny you should say that” Jeremy said… “I remember my old boss saying he came in one morning and all the weekend accounts had been filed perfectly in his ledgers… Maybe we have an inverse Poltergeist. It does good things instead of wrecking the place” he added chuckling. The inter floor intercom bleeped Tom answered it and came back. “The Artist and the Gallery Expert are here. They’re on their way up in the service elevator now… this is going to be interesting” he said.

Willaim Dean Fethersque, was a strange looking chap, he reminded Charlie of one of those Herons or Ibises. The way he walked and moved. He was carrying a valise with his authenticating tools and a Laptop case. He nearly dropped both when he saw the huge artwork

“That’s something I didn’t expect. Davis you should have warned me. We’ll need the large camera from the institute to photograph that for analysis. I’ll get on to them... Most remarkable” he said in an enthralled manner. He walked right up to the wall and took out a jewellers Loupe and examined a section of one of the Muses dresses “Incredible detail. You can make out the number of threads in the weave. Such fine brush strokes. Oh; by the way that signature is genuine. I’ve seen enough fakes to tell the difference immediately. It’s definitely by that artist. Though I can recall no mention of such a large Mural by him other than the one that’s less than half this size in the Getty Museum” he said enraptured. He ran his finger carefully across the work, gloved to protect the surface “That is amazing; it has a texture to it like Canvas. Truly remarkable” the man rang the “Institute” and had a protracted argument with the director

“If you don’t believe me I’ll send you a photo from my phone now. Though it will do the work no justice. And yes it is on Gesso. If it’s anything like the Getty one it should detach from the plaster frame but I’d be scared to try and move it without some kind of support. I’m sending you that photo next. Call me back when you decide” he said and took a picture of the Wall from the Elevator and sent it to the disbelieving Director of The Courtauld Institute. He went back up to the work and borrowed a step ladder. And used a Refractometer to get a measure of hue depth. And some other pieces of equipment to take minute measurements of brush strokes and directions. He came over to them looking puzzled “When do you think this work was done?" he asked

"It has to have been in the early thirties as this room was restructured to make way for the director's suite above. The under floor heating in that suite goes right over our heads above this ceiling. The system only came into being around that time period. And it was discontinued shortly after War broke out. Only three other buildings of a public nature have the same system" Hagan replied

"That would be what my initial analysis would say was about right. Though by this time he wasn't in this region; or so it was thought, he was in Cornwall doing a commission for the Railways. A poster design. It never got accepted though" Willaim said. And stood scratching his head. "If this follows the same construction as the Getty work, carefully putting a thin blade under the edge of that plaster covered frame should detach that from the work and the panel the Gesso is on. It only looks as if the mural goes under the frame. A very clever optical illusion that. But supporting a work of that size without it cracking will be an art in itself. The Chinese had a similar problem with some artworks in the Old Emperors Bed Chambers. And they were plaster on silk" He added. Charlie and Derek excused themselves and went to set up the Monnan for the next colour and the next plate.

The Delivery lads managed to get the units and the Dummies onto their next run with ease and they were soon being dropped off at Sadie and Robby's home. Much to the amusement of the kids, who had found a set of keys to the locked drawers in the top drawer of one of the units. The drawers contained a wealth of old advertising materials. Handouts and copies of instruction manuals for electrical products that would probably be banned as dangerously unsafe for the public these days. Some of it dated back to the late nineteen twenties. Sadie shook her head in disbelief at some of the adverts claims about some of the products. The Units only needed a good shine with a bit of furniture polish and they looked good as new. The delivery boys had found a narrower unit too and that was also delivered. That was earmarked for their son's model kit paraphernalia. And the daughter took one of the six tailor's dummies to "dress up" in her room. The extra unit was a good bonus as it meant Michael could keep his room tidy for once. Leona loved the Dummies. And even managed to get some money from two of the Women's institute seamstresses for the remaining two. The odd male one went to Charlie and Leona's bedroom to keep Charlie's old army Uniform looking right. Every time it got locked away it seemed to come out with far more creases than it went away with.

After the two had completed the artist's runs, he was called Guy Davis; they took them up to the man who they thought was still in the Haberdashery floor. The "IT" expert was doing measurements of the wall where the main Elevator was; and he came back smiling

"You're right Tom; the screen will go one side and the Interactive unit the other. And it means then that the Mural wall could take that long glass counter affair three feet from it and the access is from the front anyway, so the wall area could be roped off from the public to protect it" Lionel Watkins the IT support Technician said "The guy's had a good look at the rear of that wall and there's a false wall behind with all the electrics and the pneumatic tube delivery system. I thought those things went out with the Dinosaurs. But the exchange is behind that plywood wall in the Mailroom. Jeremy and Fred are trying to coax it back to life" he said "Oh! Hello Charlie, Derek. Those Guy Davis's runs? He's with that expert and some of them from the Courtauld Institute. You should have seen the size of that camera they used. It's back on their van. They're going over the shots on the Expert's and the Director's Laptops down in the Canteen. I'm headed there I'll take them down if you like" he added. Charlie and Derek had brought the finished prints up on one of the Mailroom's trolleys so that was easier than manually carrying them back down. They stayed up to help where they could. The space was beginning to take shape. And for some odd reason the Mural seemed to work. It certainly caught the eye and drew you into the floor.

The Glass unit Lionel had referred to was a display unit for Crystal wares and the top surface was scattered with product information leaflets and brochures. It wasn't actually Glass but Lexane, a polycarbonate material that was tough and durable. The doors even had a frame work of chromed steel. Slightly reminiscent of the Art Deco period. The lighting units in the Ceiling were actual Art Deco ones, they had been "updated" with the latest LED lighting arrays. But they worked and looked fantastic. The new wall units were white melamine with chrome trims. The Cupboards had bi-fold doors to save space. And counters were steel and thick safety glass, some frosted others not. All well-lit from within and above by requisite pendant lighting. The rear rooms that had housed a lot of the "Box Drawer" units were now a modern storage area. And there was even a mini printing room/station that customers could have prints made of pictures they had taken of products in display with their mobile devices. Or from the Software that showed the product in a room they wanted it in in their home. This was also accessed from the interactive station where Lionel's boys were putting the finishing touches to the wiring. Before "Boxing" it in and running the system for the first time.

The store was closed all day tomorrow; Sunday, for a shakedown of everything. There was a loud Shloorp sound as the Pneumatic system sprang into life. The containers had been found in among the spares in the Basement Print room and others that had been in transit ended their long overdue journeys. The Basement also had one of the tubes; they were all over the place. And more containers were found in a disused stairwell at the rear off the accounts section. That was brought back into use as it was a fast way to get to the Management Suite without being noticed using the lifts. The new store security team found that an instant hit. As it also went down to the kitchens behind the canteen. Trust them to think of their stomachs. It looked like the two of them might not be needed tomorrow. As the floor would be busy with a training exercise for the staff to "orientate" them with the new layout. While Derek chatted with Simon; Charlie took a close up look at the mural. By the signature was the faintest of marks. It looked like a very spidery pencil drawing of a pixie. But it seemed to be part of the original work. Rather than an over the top addition from a later time. The detail was really fine. Like the copperplate engraving that he'd learned to do during his apprenticeship. He still had those plates at home. He'd have to dig them out. They'd fit the Monnan perfectly. They were his indentures. And he'd taken hours putting in as much fine detail as he could manage without making the grooves so fine the ink would be too thick to allow the details to show as they would clog up. He'd done such a good job the Education Board modelled the later electronically produced images upon his plate designs.

And they'd had a lot of difficulty getting the computer to accept the detailing. An example where man could beat machine. His real indentures were in a bound folder for posterity. He went to have his lunch in the Basement with Derek.

The machines gleamed like new. The plates were soaking in the cleaning solution. They'd need a rinse and oiling with linseed oil, before storage for later runs. Guy Davis had rung him on the internal phone system; to say the quality of the runs was so good they'd do it again sometime in the near future. With the same images. A second edition set if you like. And the Bremman might be able to handle the reproduction of one of his early original works, Lady with the yellow carnation. A sort of Cubist inspired thing. Not what Charlie called art, but it takes all sorts. Derek came and joined him. He poured them both large mugs of coffee and Charlie unpacked the pile of sandwiches

"For some reason I'm really hungry today. You missed something very weird. The main overhead lights went off; some trip had gone in the wall board. But that was when someone noticed that the Muses were being lit by one of the UV lights that checks notes. I swear; as you moved across the room, the three Muses seemed to wink at you. Even that expert was surprised. They would know more when the portable X-Ray equipment arrived in an hour. That would take at least two hours to do its thing" Derek said. He'd heard of some ancient Cave paintings somewhere that exhibited an almost three dimensional quality when viewed under certain lighting conditions. A baffling quality considering how primitive the artist must have been. Charlie shook his head and they ate in silence. The Clocks thumped the next minute and that was when they heard the faint sigh. They looked at each other; then over to where the sound had originated. For a moment they thought they saw a pale blue flash of light

"Whu?" Derek said and went to investigate "Can't see what caused it, but didn't it sound like a sigh... Fred will have *me* believing in Pixies next" he added

"It was probably just a reflection from the intercom panel lights. They've been blinking on and off for weeks now. They settle themselves. The noise ... Check for an airlock in the lubricating systems of the Monnan. It happens sometimes. I should have looked at that valve a while back" Charlie said and they relaxed and enjoyed a slow lunch for once.

Classify yourself

He went by the name of Hieronymus Fidgett. He was a third class sprite if he had to classify himself, but officially... he didn't know what he was really. He'd been around for far too long if he was honest. All the others had "upped sticks" ages ago. But he, being the youngest of them, had stayed as he knew nowhere else. His parents had not taken him out on forays because he'd been a "weak child". Their way of saying an accident that shouldn't have happened. He'd been called all sorts of rude names by the others. They thought he was thick... but he was just studious enough to behave that way to avoid awkward questions. He was the last one in this place now. In this "realm of man". He'd had to learn the "job" by himself mostly so he had an excuse for not being good at it if you like. He had found a home within the current building on the site that was quiet enough for his purposes. Granted it was in the "Cellar". But where would you least expect to find someone; something, like him. Modern "Hoomans" were such vague minded things. Too much in their heads at times. Like all "young" races they tried to learn everything too quickly for their own good. Take his kind, he was still only a kid and he'd been around for several hundreds of the human's years. His kind didn't measure time in the same way. Not that it mattered really. He was the last.

He had originally "set up shop" in this building in that ruddy Time clock. But the noise made it hard to hibernate at times. Down here it was much more relaxing and sedate. Things hardly changed... Not the kind of mentality that a Muse should have. He reflected on that word and its meaning. That had changed a lot since the days of the Ladies depicted in the artwork upstairs. That Artist now... he'd been a perfect one to take instruction. "The "Muse"" he thought "An inspirational being, ethereal in quality and fixated to the point of distraction" his Dad had said "But we; some of the locals call us Pixies damn it, are among the strangest of Muses. And unlike the Ladies of ancient times, we have to remain invisible to do our work. Modern Man isn't equipped to cope with our appearance; they go all funny in their heads". He finished remembering the lecture. Dad had given it to him and his other siblings when they had all hit a certain age. Where were his parents now he wondered? He looked at the Human called Derek's "crib" notes for his upcoming "Exam". Something the "Company" expected all their younger people to take. He's made some interesting changes of late that would definitely help. But basically he was the older Human's Muse. The one called Charlie. That was the human he'd seen the spark in originally. Derek though was well on the way there now. Maybe in a few years he would have another "Charge".

He'd cursed silently when they'd had heard him sigh. And they'd almost seen him. Not good. He had set up home in the older smaller Press, because it was more his "Scale". He forgave the occasional maintenance that entailed from time to time. And took the opportunity to "explore" his "domain". That was when he'd watched the change orders being issued for the refurbishment of the Haberdashery floor. Something that was needed if he was to be honest. It had been its old layout for at least three decades now and *was* getting rather antiquated. He decided to investigate and leave the two to their meal... he rarely ate much, and in any case he "Absorbed" energy. And that was easier in the Basement than anywhere else. He had watched with growing amusement as the two humans tinkered with the old Pneumatic Delivery system. He remembered he would ride it invisible all over the building when he was a very small child. That was great fun. It would probably be as much fun today if they got it working after that ... ah; one of them spotted the problem... good. The noise it made as the blockage cleared made him almost laugh out loud. The Blockage had been a duster one of the cleaners had stuffed into one of the active vents in a vain attempt to clean the pipe. A good idea but a bad result. The pipes had removable filters to collect dust and such and the rag had ended stuck in one of the filters jamming it and the automatic shutdown system had stopped the whole thing working. Not that it mattered at that time as there were the intercoms and internal phones installed by that time.

Carriers in transit were lost in the network of pipes and these all clattered into collecting trays around the building with the "Puhfut" and "fwoop" noises associated with that. The looks of amusement as ages old orders and work notes etc. came to light was a joy to his senses. It did Humans good to look back on their past. The one called Hagan found a Message that would have gone to his grandfather from the Mailroom. It was a telegram from the Palace congratulating the store for their sterling efforts during the war. That time back then was when his next oldest brother; who was the only other Muse to stay behind, had also left. He occasionally got a message from one of the Ravens from where Blox was now. The MI6 building in London. He had been at GCHQ. He'd had some cautionary tales to tell "young" Hiram, as his name was shortened to. He put them to good use. One piece of advice was very useful. It concerned the Electricity supplies to the property. There was some new legislation in the pipeline to do with Commercial supplies. A Change in safety requirements that could make it awkward to get a direct energy absorption. He might do better to start eating solid foods again; He had; and was feeling far stronger through it. So Hiram headed to the Canteen next. He had, like most of his kind, a "sweet tooth". He raided the Sugar cube stores and some of the sandwich making supplies. He had a spot in one of the air vents he could overlook activity in the Canteen from. And he took his "rations" there. As he munched his way through them he watched the occupants below pawing over their images of the artwork. They were going to be baffled a lot by some of the features he had taught the Artist. He'd deliberately overloaded the lighting supply to show off one hidden touch he was particularly proud of.

He remembered the models the Linel had used... The Blonde was particularly sexy for a Human. Linel had ended up marrying her while they were in Cornwall. The way Humans had sex always fascinated his kind. A cousin of his still lived in an old established Brothel in Soho, London. He'd been on a visit with his Dad once. Why did

Humans complicate things? It was only a necessary part of continuing the species after all. A noise alerted him to Skizzer, the "factory" cat. A friendly animal. He had his own way of getting into the air vent system and a special way of getting between floors too. If he'd been a Human he'd have made a good Ninja or Caver. He could speak with other Animals in ways Humans had forgotten

"Hello Hiram; the Mail Room dog is at it again. Thinks I don't know and hopes the Humans will blame it on me. Yes we cats mark out territory, but not with as much as Dogs. Humans should realise that. Besides I use the litter trays provided. He has to go "walkies"" Skizzer said sarcastically "Nice to see that on display again. The Ladies do look well" he added

"Leave Bowser to me; he hates me popping up. I scare the heck out of him. I'll have him so nervous he won't be able to control himself. There's some salmon in the Basement by the large press. And a bowl of milk. Charlie looks after you well doesn't he" Hiram said and they both watched the antics as the first power up of the new units on the Elevator wall were switched on

"Hah! Typical Human's they seem to build in problems to solve to show off how smart they are. I'm off for a kip. Got a promise tonight from that female over by the Post office" Skizzer said and departed. Hiram continued to watch the chaos then he too went back to the basement.

Derek and Charlie were finishing their lunch and there were a good number of sandwiches over

"Leona always over packs a lunch box. I'll take these up to Mavis in Accounts; she's in with Jeremy they are still getting used to the new accounts software. Lionel is in with them. They have probably forgotten to eat something; you know what they're like. You could look at Maisie's bike I suppose" he said to Derek who was changing out of his overalls

"That's a good Idea. I have a Mock Exam to bone up for at College, a surprise sprung on us by the Tutor" Derek replied. And he went to get his bike from the shed. The frost had cleared now and the roads were still busy with weekend traffic so he took the back lanes. Charlie looked at Skizzer

"You look like you've had a brawl with that Tom from the Butchers again. Another patch of fur out of your tail eh!" he said. The Cat looked up from eating the salmon as if to say, "That's what you think. This is that ruddy Dog in the Mail room" and went back to eating and lapping up the milk. He looked at the clock and took of his dust coat; hung it on its hook and went to the Time Card puncher. Punched his card for the overtime and went to Accounts with the rest of the sandwiches. The store was busy and not even the work in the Haberdashery floor was denting the Saturday shop for the dedicated shoppers. He was about to leave the store at the rear when Simon accosted him.

"What are you like with steam regulators?" he asked

"I know a little of the mechanics and how they operate in general. I have a miniature "Standing Engine" my old Dad built when he was young, why?" Charlie asked in return

“We might need your expertise with a Steam Truck someone has given the Club. The regulator is stuck and it’s a totally different arrangement to the ones used on Steam Trains. Can you take a look over to the old Station some time?” he asked almost pleading

“I’ll see if Leona will let me; I think she has plans for us visiting her Cousin in Carlisle” Charlie answered

“That’s even better, that’s where the Truck is at. We only have the motor unit Diagrams from the Manufacturers Archive here. It’s the Old Goods Yard at Carlisle Station and Bernie is stopping there with a Friend of his. You could kill two birds with one stone… What d’you says?” He looked pleadingly

“I’ll … No I’d be bored to tears at Elsie’s so why not; and Dennis would tag along if there’s a chance of a pint in the offing. Derek can manage on his own for a week at least… I reckon maybe longer, but Tom won’t let him yet” Charlie said. And they agreed to do that. Charlie knew Leona wouldn’t mind, Elsie wouldn’t mind either; it would get Dennis out from under her feet, and the two women could have a good natter.

A Muse in Solitary

Hiram and his brother Blox thought they were the only pair left, till a Crow called in on Blox with a message on its leg. It had come from a distant relative in Scotland everyone had thought had moved on long ago. He was on one of the Hebrides, nobody knew which exactly. It seems he was having issues with the local Humans and some new Rat Traps they were employing. A ship had wrecked and the Rats had made their way to shore. The Island was so remote that the ferry only came once every three months. And a Ministry fella had told the Locals that Warfarin wouldn't work on them rats. His Name was Hamish Donegal. A Muse like Hiram and Blox he was married and his mate had moved on a week ago. She should be in the London Area by now. He just wanted her back if it was possible. Hiram had established a sort of Muse Telephone to tap into the national networks between him and Blox. Blox had called him with the news about Hamish

"His mate is called Whisper. And from what the Ravens tell me; she's set up in the White Tower. Effectively in Solitary so to speak. She and Hamish had some kind of spat as to how to handle the locals' Rat problem... And she being a former Hunderson... well you know how stubborn that family were. It might be better if Hamish moves here" Blox said. Hiram agreed. They were the last and had to stick together.

"He could do worse. And least they'd have a "Castle" to keep" Hiram said. Aware of the awful puns. It made Blox laugh "Any message we send is going to take at least a month to see having any effect. We are a rare breed and we should be together ... or closer together at least" Blox said and the line cut as he severed the tap. He let Blox draught the message and a Herring Gull took it to Hamish for them. In the meantime as Blox was closer he was going to seek out Whisper and get her side of things. The Last Muse at The Tower had been a female too. And *she* always spoke *highly* of the Tower Guards *and* the living conditions. So being in Solitary might not be as bad as it sounded. He was to concentrate on that Expert and the people from the Courtauld Institute. They could prove to be a problem.

He was to be alone in the Basement tomorrow, so he took it upon himself to do a little extra maintenance of the larger press in there. He had technical manuals that Blox had managed to send to the Store disguised as free samples of magazines etc. He would let Derek and Charlie have access to them by surreptitiously leaving them in a corner cupboard. Speaking of which... the Units were being brought in. A lot more than Charlie may have thought. And the weird mobile ladder system to access the higher stacked box drawers. He watched from the vantage point of the air vent as the units were brought in minus their drawers. Once a bottom unit was fastened in place the upper one was positioned and the rail the ladders ran along attached to the top of the upper unit; and that unit was also fastened securely to the wall. Then as the next sections were fitted the previous ones were kitted out with the drawers. He might help Charlie and Derek out by putting some of the more common parts in drawers and labelling the drawers for them. This time he would print the Labels using that new printer in the Accounts office. It was going to be empty tomorrow too. He went through the vents to where the Expert and the Courtauld crew were discussing something with the artist Guy Davis. He got as close as he dared

"... Surprisingly his widow is still around and their kids. The Daughter Mantra has taken up the mantle of artist in the family. The sons are engineers, one in the Navy. I have an appointment with Mantra at her studio in Durham in the Northeast. Next month after my Exhibit in the Tate" Guy was saying

“I hope she has access to her father’s archives... The Institutes and the History Museum records are sketchy at best” Willaim said

“See what you can glean Mr Davis... Now what do you make of those pigments used that react in the UV spectrum... I thought the minerals were only found in Umbria” One of the Courtauld technicians said

“That’s what you think sunshine” Hiram thought to himself “There are sources all over if you know where to look. And we Muses do” he added under his breath as quietly as possible.

“They are still picking at the artwork are they” Skizzer said as he came to watch also “Bowser is off with Jennifer from Lingerie. She’s “looking after him when he comes out of the Vets... Poor thing he won’t know where to hide his face when the anaesthetic wears off” the cat said

“Ouch! When was that decided? Still he’ll be out of our hair a while. And tender no doubt when he does come back. Jennifer lives in Milton Keynes doesn’t she?” Hiram asked

“Yes as far as I know. She loves to tickle my tummy and she does always smell nice” Skizzer said as he went off to do his many “Cat” related things. The sound of him scrabbling about in the Vents got a few puzzled looks from below, but nobody investigated when Fred said...

“Probably a couple of Pigeons again, the bloody devils get in somewhere I have yet to find out where though. Found a pair of Kestrels nesting by the Air Conditioners last week". And they all shrugged and continued their debate. Hiram went back to the Basement and the work had been completed and the lads were cleaning up. Charlie and Derek's boxes of bits waiting for their attention. The place looked a lot more efficient now. And the Paper Stock Cupboard had been better laid out too. That would help Charlie. He went into the now empty Print Room and retrieved his tools and tackled the optical sensors that aligned the over printing synchronisation in the Bremman this, not the old electronics of the Matrices, was the cause of the periodic slip in alignment. When he finished the Optics were crystal clear and the emitters were changed. The aging units left with a Note to be put on the Logs. When he'd finished it was approaching evening. The lad's had forgotten to turn off the lights. So he went to his own switch board and did the honours. He had become quite the electronics genius of late. The relays hidden in the wiring latched open and the lights went out. He'd reset them early in the morning; just before Fred opened up. He was always the first in. Though it was Sunday so he would leave it a little later than usual. It would give the Humans something to wonder about when they came on after the trip boxes were checked and found OK. A little mystery is to be expected in life after all. As it happened Blox would come to see him with a visitor.

Charlie had been right about Leona and Elsie. The journey was going to be in Robby's car. The plan was to set off early and head west and up the coast then back inland and up to Carlisle. Robby, Sadie and the kids were going to a nearby attraction and then when they were ready to go back, a quick call to pick the couple up and they'd take a motorway route back. It would be a good day out for the kids; and the adults could have a bit of peace while the kids tired themselves out. That was the plan... As it turned out, a different arrangement soon surfaced that was actually more expedient. And it left Robby and Sadie and their two free to do as they pleased. Charlie had forgotten about a little perk available to all the older staff at Hamptons General store. Paid for Excursions. And it didn't take long to organise one for the staff and their partners. It was to be a sort of Mystery tour lasting two days with overnight stays in accommodations. With a bit of jiggery pokery, Simon had "tweaked" the itinerary to the destination being Carlisle. The women in the tour group would have shopping vouchers; the men would have some other arrangement. So Charlie and Bernie could meet up without arousing suspicion and Leona and Elsie could spend time together with Leona doing a shop for Christmas presents. As long as he didn't get "mucked up" she was OK with that. It also meant Sadie and the Kids could go to Alton Towers instead. Even Robby enjoyed being there, so everything was set. Charlene and the kitchen girls were traveling together with her Hubby and two of the Men's Outfitters male counter staff Daniel and Fergus. And you could bet a bottom dollar they would sneak some booze on board the coach. So there may be some impromptu toilet stops along the way no doubt. They would save a case for the Driver for him to savour later. Works tours were rare in the modern day workplace, but Hamptons had always prided itself with keeping up traditions. Even Hagan and Adora his missus were coming along.

In the Store all was quiet for the Evening. When the other Muse and his visitor arrived. They were surprised to be escorted by a cat. Hiram introduced Skizzer. Whisper was younger than Hiram had expected. And very attractive for a "Pixie". Even she hated that term; when Hiram told her about Fred and his former Bosses fixation

"And they don't suspect you are here?" she said incredulously

"So far only Skizzer; Bowser and the birds know about me. This store is quite a place to cover for one Muse. If we could persuade Hamish to come here. Maybe there could be an arrangement to rotate the places from time to time" Hiram suggested

"I am not sure Hamish would agree. He's very set in his ways. And the locals are less than a nuisance at times. Not a spark between them" she said. Ah; there it was, When a Muse had no charge they got complacent and stuck

"If he came here on a visit; or to London, I dare say he'll find a spark or two. What was his "speciality"?" Blox asked

"He was a Farming Muse originally, and then an artist took his eye. They moved to the Hebrides to get inspiration for landscape works. The Charge he was watching over on the island after the Artist went; passed a decade ago; and he just went cold. Why he didn't just move on or seek a new Charge is something he won't open up about. It was one of the reasons of our "disagreement". I had lost my Musical Charge, she was a brilliant Harpist. And I was wandering when I came across him alone on the island. I tried; but..."Whisper said "Not good for a Muse to be so long without" she added. Hiram knew how that could go from an Uncle who lost his inspiration power. Through lack of drive. That Uncle went the way of the unloved; unworshipped Gods... The realm beyond the end of time. A huge void. It was reasoned that something went wrong in creation and the Void was what was left of all that was planned. An Error of such a minute degree can have immense consequence. Hamish looked like he was heading to that Void

“The Gull should have made it there by now” Blox said. Sure enough the next day a Crow from the Island sent a return message

“I need my Lass; tell her I’m sorry and I’m on my way” Blox read. A start at least.

The Sunday was madness at first; but soon the training was settling down, only the staff that would be in the refurbished department were in for training. The final fitting and testing of the new systems was done as they went through their paces. And a thorough test of the Pneumatic system was also being done. It gave the Muses the opportunity to traverse the entire Store almost invisibly. But they had to move fast to avoid someone seeing them and that would cause all sorts of problems and questions

“This is the thrill I missed” Whisper said “If we can get Hamish into this kind of environment; especially where the young are, he’ll recover. I’m sure of it” she added. They got a Message via a Rat that Hamish had turned up in the rear Yard and was hiding in the Equipment stores. They headed over. Hamish was actually quite tall for a Muse of their kind. He had been so even as a child. He was very nervous and didn’t know what to make of Skizzer. The local feral cats and rats on the Island were evil buggers and were always causing him grief. It took an hour before he felt comfortable around the cat

"Och! Ken he's a friend and all that... But I still get the willikers when ah sees him" he said as he hugged Whisper with tears streaming down his cheeks. He cheered up no end by evening; especially after a few rides of "The Tubes" as he called them. He'd been in a Department Store in Edinburgh in his childhood with his Parents. They'd had the same system and he enjoyed riding it. This brought back memories. Hiram and the others felt the Imagination drive returning. It was the late evening and all the staff and the refurb crew were getting ready to depart when they spotted it. Hamish had seen a spark. And he was fixated on the holder of that spark. One of the young Female Counter staff

"She's got it strong this one" he said "And Ah sense she'll gan far. If she can get her head around where she's at" he added

"Lucy Kenmore she's called" Hiram said and told all of them about her tragic story. She had been orphaned young and an aunt and Uncle had brought her up in Yorkshire. She had moved here to Manchester when they died and went to college. She studies Art there and from what she showed the other women from time to time; she was a natural. But circumstances being what they were. One of her older brothers took her in

"You might know him Whisper, he's a Guard at the Tower. She is allowed to stay with him when she's in London. She is thinking of going to live in London when she Graduates." He said. Hamish looked to be thinking hard on the idea.

Monday came and the store soon got busy. Hamish really was fixated on Lucy. Kept sending ideas and suggestions. Some got through others didn't

"Och! She's wayward in the concentration" he said when they were in the vent above the canteen eating lunch

"Hamish... I have to get back to my charges in the Tower. They are into Barber Shop music; some are really good singers. She visits in a week, come with her. There's a good service that's easy to follow comes right close. And if ye say when ye coming; I'll meet ye" Whisper said; and Blox and her set off

"Ah dinna ken why she stays tight tae me. She can dee better ye ken" Hamish said when she went

"You should think yourself lucky; no woman has come my way for a century or more. I'm older than I look" Hiram said in return. They were watching a couple of children who seemed fascinated by the artwork on the wall. Awe struck in fact.

"I ken thae Artist. He came up oor way wance. Stayed in Edinburgh afore heading to Cornwall. He was an odd'un. I suppose ye were his Muse then?" Hamish quizzed

"Yes; and a few others. I'm really Old Charlie's Muse these days. He's away on a works tour. I have a memory glass I can show you. And that young Apprentice of his is coming to the fore too. So I'm kept busy. I also help a Fay that's set up at the Canal. She's a bit too brassy for my liking" Hiram said and took him to his Archive.

Fays were another of the Faery folk. Closely related and it was possible for the two kinds to interbreed; but they rarely did so, Fays were also rare in Urban areas. More associated with wilderness places or forests. Like Nymphs they were Water Sprites. Fays tended to be solitary for most of their lives. Nymphs were far *too* gregarious. The Memory Glass to which Hiram referred was the principal means that a Muse had of recording permanently; a Charges progress. He had a large collection in his Archive. Not really glass but a transparent mineral with an extremely high refractive index. It took on thought waves like a sponge takes on water. The volume dictated the length of the memory recordable. To replay the memory; you had to trigger the appropriate thread of thought that set it in the first place. A permanent way of keeping track of Multiple Charges and a useful tool for teaching younger Muses the trade. Charlie's Memory Glass was a cube about three inches square. All the six faces portrayed various aspects of Charlie's tutelage by Hiram. Hamish watched and chuckled occasionally

"He's got a good heart that one; if a little crude at times" He said, losing his accent and imitating Hiram

"Aye, he has a that" Hiram returned the favour. They had a good laugh with each other

"Wheer's this "Servis" Whisper's ane aboot?" He asked "I feels inspired tae visit" he added. That was what Hiram wanted to hear. He said Skizzer would take him; if he didn't mind riding Bareback on a Cat. Hamish wasn't as pensive about Skizzer after he'd seen how good a ratter he was

“Nae problem. He’s a rare one that beastie. And it beats air travel… Birds can get awfy incontinent ye ken?” he said. Hiram got the gist of that easily enough and said

“Draughty too”…

In at the Deep end

Charlie and Derek came in on Tuesday early to set up the presses to do some runs of the Special Wrapping Papers the Bremman for the larger sheets, the Monnan for the smaller sheets. It would be a test of the cutting assembly on the Bremman. The blade was a rotary one and had been stuck solidly in place. The maintenance had not only freed it; but had highlighted a problem. When the press had been installed all those decades ago; someone had mounted it on the wrong side of the machine. Now correctly mounted it shouldn’t jam up or tear the sheets as it had done in the past. The blade should last a little longer too. There wasn’t such a problem with the Monnan. Being single sheet at a time auto feed. And the designs required only one colour on the plates. So they could be pre-inked and changed when the Input stock was changed. They even had a plate for boxes. The Monnan had six different plates with six different patterns. Each with a central panel depicting an image of the old store frontage and the name. The Bremman could be reprogrammed with around a hundred or so designs on plug in “Font” cartridges. And the fonts could be altered between sheets if needed.

The roll; about a foot in diameter and as wide as A0 could be fitted and changed with ease on the Bremman. And the order was for A3 wide. Those rolls were a larger diameter. And it took two people to mount them. The rolls dropped into a hopper with two rotating rollers and the paper end came out between these and was grabbed by a third which then fed it into the input rollers and the auto feeder. It saved a lot of "threading up". They had an order for fifty sheets twice A3 length of three designs in four single colours. That was two hundred in total; and a hundred of the Mail Coach Winter scene in full colour; for the lingerie department. They were using those sheets for special orders. They were for the Bremman. The Monnan was doing the single sheets of A1 for the other departments and that meant two hundred of each. It was going to be a busy day; and Derek hadn't done this job before. It was going to be a case of "in at the deep end" for him. Surprisingly he was doing great… so far. Wait till the second roll change.

Simon and his buddies had been really pleased with the help Charlie had given with the regulator. It was a mechanical problem that was down to incorrect assembly. It wasn't clear from the diagrams where two parts should have been and these had got transposed. The thing was trying to act in reverse. So he didn't get "Mucked up" much and his hands were easily cleaned. He hadn't seen the kind of disposable paper overalls the enthusiasts used. And asked the name of the supplier. It would be useful to have some for summer; when it could get as hot as an oven sometimes in the Basement print room. Leona said he should order some for his garage at home; when he finally met up with the rest of the Works outing lot. They were in a Bar having an impromptu break in shopping. He only wanted a few items he could get easily before the coach driver called time to go back. Elsie called him over

“That young apprentice lad you have; does he ever wear Canvas shoes?” she asked

“I’ve seen him wear them from time to time... Why?” Charlie had asked. When she told him the answer to that; he nearly fell off the barstool he was on.

In the Print room they left the Monnan to print the first two hundred of one colour and watched the registration on the Bremman. They’d both seen the spidery hand written Log and the note about the Optical. Why hadn’t they thought of that? Whoever the mysterious helper was had been absolutely spot on. The registration was far truer even on the single colour runs. When they eventually did the full colour runs the results were perfect every time

“I’m going to read the Manuals on servicing that part of the press, and the Cutter. It hasn’t split the blade so far, like it used to do every fifty on heavy bonds” Derek said

“Er! I noticed you wear Canvas shoes from time to time, Nike brand aren’t they?” Charlie said

“Yeah! I have an issue sometimes with my feet and the blood vessels. Especially on hot days. That’s why I have three pairs of each colour I wear. One being cleaned; one to change into and the other I’m wearing. And I can’t seem to get away with wearing even them tiny Trainers socks though” He replied as he made a slight adjustment to the Monnan in the angle of the feed tray to accommodate the reducing stack of stock. It was a weight balancing system and they’d had it set for heavier bond than they were using. Not that the Monnan minded one jot. It just plodded along

“Only; Leona’s Cousin Elsie has some older styles from Nike that an Uncle left behind when they emigrated to Australia. She thought they might be collectable and wondered if you’d like them. There’s about eighteen pairs in the store locker at the Gym her Hubby co-runs. Would you be interested?” he asked

“Probably; though the real money is in the Trainers and the Celebrity links. Air Jordan’s of a particular era and in unused; boxed condition go for some real silly money these days. The Shoes are not as collectible; but if they’re a Designer model from the seventies, we could be talking four hundred to seven hundred… depending on the size; some sizes are not so popular” Derek said as he left the Monnan.

“I’m taking a break; I suggest you do. That roll will need changing in an hour on the Bremman and you’ll need your strength. The replacement roll is a heavier bond” Charlie said”

“Fine by me. I’ll try some sketching from the Gallery over the Central Shop floor. I’ll not be in the way up there. And the angle should make the drawings look more interesting” he said and left. Charlie didn’t dare tell him that there was a pair of Gold and Black Air Jordan’s in that shoe collection… he’d probably have dashed up to Carlisle as fast as he could on the Motorbike of his. Besides the delivery boys could bring them back from their next run up there next week.

Hiram had been watching from a vent near to the Pneumatic Pipe to the Accounts department and the “in Tray”. He noted where the lad was going and realised the vent on the floor above was straight up the pipe above him and off three feet to the left. He scrambled up and almost caught Skizzer in a very sore spot

"Steady; I had a fight with a large Rat last night, down by the Canal. They're getting altogether too clever of late. One of them trapped my tail in a mouse trap" the disdainful tabby said "And that Hamish didn't Help matters by calling all the Gulls that name he uses for vermin. I had to go to a fountain to get the crap out of my fur. And you know how I hate it when the Girls in the Kitchen give me a bath" he complained

"I wouldn't want to meet that rat in a hurry" Hiram said as he settled to watch and hopefully inspire Derek

"He's getting awfully good he is; and that Rat... Well put it this way; he won't be siring any more young" he said. And Skizzer flexed his claws. Hiram winced.

A Fay comes to roost

Word came that afternoon that Hamish was enjoying being in the Tower. And he had found six promising sparks already. Blox has found another charge and was moving to Manchester to be with him so would be a lot closer. Things seemed to be looking up. He knew now he wasn't the last Muse. The two of them watched Derek draw. Neither of them had realised the time passing when the vibration made them start

"Oh Damn it. The heating cycler. I hope we have time to get to the over flow exhaust. Quick Skizzer." Hiram said and they departed to a secondary system as fast as they could. While Blox had been visiting Hiram; he had found an old disused part of the Pneumatic Delivery system and had made it operational for use in getting across the store in an emergency. The container was too small for Skizzer; but the vent system where they were at also had a way down to the Basement that could be shut off from the main system if need be. Hiram saw Skizzer into the right vent pipe and on his way before closing the diverter gates to redirect the hot air flow. Before finally getting away in the container across the space above the ground floor entrance. The pipe then arced around and went down to the Garage for the delivery trucks. He could use the old venting pipes to get back into the Basement. He looked at the completed piles of wrapping papers; a couple of extras of each had been used to wrap the piles with to keep them clean; and tidy till needed. Charlie had roped in one of the Mail room boys to help load them onto one of their trolleys to be taken to Packaging. That gave Derek a little more time. He was looking through some of the Old Catalogues that the Store used to produce.

Tom had come down to have his lunch in peace and quiet. Besides he enjoyed Charlie's company to some of the noisy lot in the Canteen

"I remember them being put in huge piles in the foyer behind the two rotating doors; so that customers could pick up a copy. The covers were always seasonal. We don't do that anymore; a real shame. You remember the look on the kids' faces when they saw what was going to come to the Toy department" he said

"Only too well. I remember when the then Manager old Gregson decided they were too "old fashioned" and stopped us printing them. He almost killed the preseasonal sales with that move" Charlie replied

"I saw Derek in the Gallery as I came down. He's getting bloody good at his detailing. I'm toying with the idea of having him do some designs for a series of Hampton's own Postcards. We'd print them here; the Lasers would look too crisp, and sell them as packaged sets with the seasonal stamps and first covers that come out every Christmas and such. Tell him to come by with some of his other sketches he's already got. I'll have the management team send someone too. If the likes of Harrod's and Christies can do it why not Hamptons?" Tom said

"I reckon Derek might be up for that. As long as he completed his apprenticeship with me here first. At least then when I retire; the company will have someone who knows the place inside out" Charlie agreed "and there's something else I found while I was clearing out and reorganising the Stock Cupboard. A stack of unused Saving Stamps from the old Saver's scheme the shop used to have… It could be revived in time for the customers to start saving now for next Christmas; Easter or whatever. Putting toward a big Hamper for example. It helped considerably post war" Charlie added

"Everywhere seems to be on a nostalgia trip of late… you might be onto something there" Tom replied "But I wonder if we could come up with something that would be nostalgic and totally Hamptons own?" he added. Hiram had watched all this. Tom in his way was a spark; but the kind Hiram couldn't nurture… His Sister when she was around could have. It was a different skill set to his… then he remembered the Fay. He had a Crow take her a message explaining. He didn't get a reply until a Cat from the Canal Feral crew turned up. Skizzer would have nearly killed him for invading his turf till he saw the special kind of message paper it had fastened to its left front leg

"Steady on Skizzer. I saw what you did to that rat. I don't want the same. I'm here on a mission for the Fay at the canal site. It's for your Muse. Besides. I'm thinking of leaving The Ferals... They are getting far too wild for my liking. Maybe I'm getting old; but I can see that lot sending me to the bottom of the canal one day with their antics" the cat, called Ginge said

"I'll take you to him. You know; I think that Fay has the hots for Hiram... But you can't tell with them. Not like our females" Skizzer replied and took Ginge to meet with Hiram "Besides you might be able to help me out with some Gulls ...they roost in one of the old wharf buildings I'm certain. I hate having baths more than being shat on by stupid birds. And they need a paying back" he added as they took the freight lift down to the basement. The Mail room was loading an afternoon delivery and unloading the returned packaging from the electricals installation crew for recycling. So the cats went unnoticed and Hiram met them in the Stock Cupboard out of sight and earshot. The Fay's reply was surprising to say the least. The Canal ran past where Tom lived. She had seen his spark and would be more than willing to help. But she was a Water Fay and needed to be near to water to replenish. At his home it would not be a problem... But there at work... he'd be "in the dry zone" as she put it. Hiram thought about this and it suddenly dawned on him. The Arboretum at the store's west road entrance had a large cascade fountain. It was always on and operating as it was part of the Humidity system for the plants used there. He gave Ginge a note to go back.

“Was I seeing things or did Ginge have a birthmark like a crow?” Hiram asked

“I’d spotted that too. The only other cats I’ve seen with that birthmark were… it couldn’t possibly be… But the family left for America a decade ago. Took their cats with them. He must have been one of the kittens that was meant to have drowned. Unauthorised litter the humans called it. The mother was pedigree; The Ferals must have taken him in. I wonder if he knows he’s related to Cat Royalty” Skizzer said.

A day later Gardenia Hopkiss, the Fay arrived riding on Ginge’s back. With a small suitcase. She was moving in. There was going to be a “clean up” and dredging of the canal and that could have been very bad if she was seen. She had also helped Ginge get out of The Ferals

“Hello Hiram. Which way is this Fountain? And is there some place I can set up shop nearby?” she asked

“I’ll show you; and Skizzer, you have something to say to Ginge don’t you. Take the suitcase to the West corridor “C” Storage cupboard. The one that’s not used anymore.” He instructed “And nobody will bother you there.. I got all the keys away from them. Besides they have so many storage places in here they never use that one anymore. Too far to walk most of the time. So you’ll not be seen or disturbed. And from the ceiling vent there it’s a straight passage to the vent in the Arboretum and that fountain. But we are going to take a different route” he said mysteriously and offered Gardenia his arm, all gentleman like. She laughed and took it and the two headed over to the disused pipe of the Pneumatic Delivery system. They climbed into the container and were whisked away over the system to the depositing tray of the West Road side of the store. From there it was a short walk to the Arboretum

"I can get used to that thing. And we can meet each other regularly. If I remember what your message said about Tom... he has an Office up on the next floor from here. I'd like to see that place. I have a feeling that it will be close enough to this huge fountain for me to keep replenished all the time. Does anyone come round here nights?" she asked

"No; not at night, except me, Skizzer and Blox when he's here. He likes to Skinny dip in the fountain. Skizzer hates the idea of bathing... Most cats do" Hiram answered

"Blox... I met him once oh all of twenty years ago. I was in London doing a tour of the City water features. A sort of regular blessing ritual. He's a fine figure of a man; if a little coarse for my liking" she said as she followed Hiram to where Tom's Office was sited

"The vent in there joins with the others from the far side of the store and to my area in the Basement. And there's the Service corridors down stairs on the ground floor that interconnect. Only the Electricians use them at night; and then rarely. I use one of the Toy Cars from the Toy department to get around in those corridors" Hiram said

"I am very close to water here; Are those water pipes?" she asked pointing to a cluster of pipes running up and down a wall

“Oh of course they are the heating pipes. The boiler and pumps are in the Boiler room in the Basement area below here. There’s a lot more water in this place than I thought” he said chuckling. He’d remembered saying that he thought the place would be too arid for her

“I only have to be near water… but the idea of bathing in that fountain is becoming quite … Ooh I reckon that might be a good idea. You’re not shy are you?” she asked. Hiram felt himself blush a deeper shade of blue

“I could adapt a schedule so you can have alone time to do that” he said She laughed

“Relax; I’m only teasing you. I’d warn you in advance when I’m thinking of doing that. Take it Tom doesn’t think of himself as a writer then… Those cards you sent with that Crow; that he wrote the verses for say otherwise. Getting a concept and an emotion across in a limited number of words takes a real writers skill. I can work with talent like that. And it’s been some time since any lovesick poets have come to the Canals” she said. He took her to the Storage Cupboard he’d mentioned and she did a ritual protection casting. “This place feels good; it’s got history and foundation. The very basis of a lasting hope… I may leave the Canal for good. The Humans will take it over again. It’s going to be some kind of municipal park. And I can’t be having kids throwing too many coins in the fountains. This one has a different feel to it… A clean feel. Yes; I can be at home here” she said. And surprised the cats and kissed Hiram. Skizzer and Ginge had a laugh when Hiram turned bright blue and pulsed.

edition of Winnie The Pooh. Did Derek illustrate this?" he'd asked. Derek was blushing when he confirmed he had "Don't be like that boy; these are excellent, and you have the scenes and the characters just like I would imagine them to be. And I recognise the faces of some from the staff here" he said "The uppers want me to have my Portrait Photo taken for the Gallery in the Directors boardroom... Hang that. Derek I want you to draw me and sign it. Confound the old farts. Wha do you say?" he asked

"I'd be honoured" was all that Derek could muster. Hiram was pleased as punch for the lad. There had been an underhanded side to Hagan's suggestion; and that would come to light later.

Hamish and Whisper departed on Ginge and Skizzer to the service and this time Hamish didn't upset the Gulls; in fact they steered clear of pair of Tom Cats

"What did you do to them Ginge?" Skizzer asked as they dropped off their riders in time to catch the train

"Well The Gulls here have a memory of when the place got fire bombed during the war; it's passed down through the generations. And the smell of burning feathers gets them in a right panic. I threatened to have the roost firebombed, they panicked and now they keep well out of the way whenever I'm around on my prowls. And there is a chance I could get it done" Ginge said and nodded at a Chinese Takeaway rear entrance

"I know that owner; he has ... He's got insurance on that building. He set fire to one of his own restaurants or so the Authorities reckoned; but they found little evidence to prove so, so he got a massive insurance pay-out… How would you get him to do the job?" Skizzer asked bemused

"Easy… he's not a Human, he's a Bogeyman. One of the new breed that's into cleanliness. And Gull and Pigeon droppings are an anathema to them… he'd burn the place down to get rid of the stuff" Ginge said

"A Bogeyman? I thought they went out into the Countryside; as Town was getting too "clean" for them" Skizzer said as they headed back.

"Not this new lot; young you see, always rebel against their parents. He even married a Human just to spite his old Dad; and lives like one too got a kid on the way so would need the extra cash" Ginge said… they made the Shop Yard just as the last of the Security staff finished their early rounds.

The Print room looking Spic and span in no time; Hiram and Gardenia went their separate ways. They had agreed to meet for lunch in the vent overlooking the Canteen. A water pipe ran above the vent to feed the sprinklers. Gardenia had found that Hamptons had set up a cookery demonstration to show off a new rage of cooking equipment; and there was a surplus of baked goods left that the public had not taken as "Samples". She found some vol au vent cases and some savoury meat paste; High energy food for the hard working pair. Inspiring a charge could be energy sapping sometimes; other times the feedback could over charge the Muse. Swings and roundabouts. Hiram had found some Coffee flavoured milk drinks and a large Tea urn that he could fill some thimble flasks from. They used Dolls pottery from the Toy Department to serve everything in and on. There was a small wooden flat topped music box that served as a table. They sat looking over the lunching Humans and became so engrossed they didn't hear the scraping noise from the lower parts of the Air vents... When they did Hiram cursed"

"It's the Maintenance inspection thing. A sort of Mobile camera' Grab the table and put it behind that panel and go behind it. I'll go up through my escape hatch and we'll wait till it's gone. The Humans operate it remotely. If they see us... I dread to think what might happen" he cautioned

Gardenia and he pushed the table away like he'd said and he clambered up into the escape hatch. The cover for this was a mesh grille that was originally meant to have a Sensor behind for the Fire detection system. But was left out and repositioned elsewhere. He could watch the thing and not be visible. Too late he realised he'd dropped his spare tool bag. His heart pounded as the crawling robot camera thing came in to inspect the Vent. It was a newer model than before; but operated the same way. It was smaller and more compact to squeeze into tighter spaces. In the vent it looked like a toy. From a peep hole left by the removal of a fastening screw Gardenia eyed the thing. It seemed to have a sort of fidgeting movement to it. And the camera now swivelled around on top of the body. The Tracks were magnetic and the body had some Vacuum enable Suction cups that could hold the thing on vertical surfaces while the operators scanned the area with the camera. Thankfully the thing had actually parked over Hiram's tool bag so it wasn't visible to the camera. The operators must have been satisfied with what they had seen and the thing;

camera pointing in the other direction reversed out of the vent. They heard the thing go down to the junction below and head off in the direction of the Arboretum network of vents when the noises had gone they both emerged

"That was close. One of these days something like that is going to catch one of us. Then all hell will break loose" Hiram said"

"Those silly Drone things are more likely to spot us. The Toy Department has set up a display in the Arboretum because of the height of the place. I saw what those things are like down at the Canal. They are bloody fast and very manoeuvrable. They can't use them in these steel vents though the control signals mustn't be able to get in to them" Gardenia said. He'd forgotten that the area by the Canal had a training spot where Drone pilots could "hone their Skills" without causing interference to the other members of the general public.

"When did they set that up?" he asked

"Oh this morning around ten. The kids were eager and there was a scramble to be the first. Some of the Adults were just as bad" she replied giggling "One Father took on his own son in a "Dog Fight" and lost miserably... He looked like he was going to burst into tears" she added and laughed a little too loudly. The hubbub in the canteen ceased

"Keep it down I think they heard you?" Hiram hissed quietly. Hearing no more the Humans in the Canteen went back to what they were doing

“Sorry I keep forgetting these vents sort of amplify the sounds we make. Uh oh! I think my charge has got a sort of block. I need to fluence him… But I’m too far here. Where would he go next?” she asked

“Tom would probably go to the Arboretum to check on the sales in the boutiques around the space; then up to his office” Hiram answered

“Does that sky light above the Arboretum open up?” She asked next

“Yes there’s a control near the light switch by the elevator. You’d need some kind of ladder to get up to it though” he answered

“I’ll work that out when I get there. The pigeons come back around an hours’ time… That’s when the next demonstration time is for the drones… I think I can give Tom a visual stimulus to get his creative juices flowing again” she said and tapped the side of her nose. Hiram had a bad feeling about this.

Later; Gardenia managed to get a moment to open the Skylight using some stilts from the toy department. She was inventive; Hiram gave her that, and he went to her spot in the vent in the Upper gallery of the Arboretum. There should have been trees in this place; but instead a large water feature had been built instead. When the windows in the skylight were open; the splashing waters of the fountain attracted birds of every description, more so the sparrows and pigeons. Pigeons being greedy birds by nature; they investigated a scattering of seeds that Gardenia had placed. Tom heard the commotion outside and came out to see a pitched battle between the Pigeons and the Sparrows. Over the seed and some scraps. It must have done something to Tom's mind and he; instead of getting furious, laughed and went back into his office. The frenzied sound of typing brought a smile to Gardenia's face and the Janitor and the crew inspecting the vents gave the shoppers a hilarious sight; Derek was there with a sketch pad capturing the scene of the men trying to catch the birds or shoo them out of the skylights. Hiram shook his head and thought to himself "If it works I suppose...But she's going to get caught; or get both of us caught. Skizzer joined in; he was having a whale of a time. Ginge was sat watching the chaos with Hiram from a hidden viewpoint

"How old is she supposed to be. That stunt is so childish" Ginge said

"You're telling me...Here comes the culprit now" Hiram said scowling as Gardenia joined them

"That was fun, and you should see Tom now, writing like a demon... And it looks like Derek's having a good time too" She said chuckling

"You do realise we could be caught pulling stunts like that." Hiram admonished

"I'm surprised at Skizzer he's old enough to know better... Look at him; he's behaving like a kitten in a Wool box" Ginge added. Skizzer eventually gave up and spotted them with his keen eyesight and made a beeline to where they were

"I haven't had that much fun in ages. I managed to clip a

few of the flying rats. And I think I caught one with a wound. There's blood spatter. I'm surprised you didn't have a go Ginge" Skizzer said and looked shamefaced at the look he got from Hiram. They say a woman foot tapping in anger can worry the wildest of beasts. Well Gardenia was at the receiving of a crossed set of arms and a foot tapping from Hiram. Then to complete the set... The voice; Called the "Weirding Way", it was an ancient method of controlling a subject tightly, issued from his lips. It wasn't so much what he said... The Voice hammered it home. And he stalked off to calm down. He rode the Pipes to the basement.

Charlie was reading then sports section of the paper and filling in his Pools Coupon. He walked behind him to his hidey hole at ground level

"It's no use sulking" Charlie said. Hiram froze. Charlie was looking at him "And don't look that horrified. I know all about the little folk from my Gran" he added. It wasn't good for a charge to see his Muse. It could break the bond and cause all sorts of problems

"You... Know about me?" Hiram said puzzled enough to stay visible

"Yes! But I thought it best to let you make the first move. I was still waiting till I saw the footage from one of those Drone thingies. For some reason that old portable TV in my "Office" picks up the camera signals. You and the other one were almost caught by the Crawler in the Vents this morning too" Charlie answered

"And you're fine with seeing me?" Hiram said back; completely perplexed now

“I shouldn’t be I suppose. It’s you keeps the presses shining isn’t it?” Charlie asked. Hiram confirmed. “Nobody will be down here for an hour. Hop up here and let’s talk” Charlie added... Ginge peeked around the door and froze for a moment; but Hiram’s peripheral vision had caught him

“Oh! Rats! Ginge has spotted us... That’s going to cause ructions. I just gave the most powerful lecture on keeping from being seen too” and Hiram slumped. Ginge didn’t run to the others though. But sauntered in and sat looking at them.

If anybody *had* been around; they would have thought they were going mad... Cats don’t talk and little blue men don’t exist and for both to be having a conversation with an old man... They would have signed the certificate then and there themselves. Charlie had surmised some things wrong; but he did seem to have a good idea of the way things actually were and worked.

“It’s unusual for a Charge to actually feel his Muse influence them... How long have you suspected?” Hiram eventually asked. Derek was heading down in the elevator. The TV had tapped into the shops internal CCTV cameras and he was spotted entering the Elevator in Haberdashery and that was headed to ground level.

“He’s another of your “Charges” isn’t he?” Charlie asked

“Yes; but I don’t think he suspects. He’s real Spark and no mistake. So are you for that matter” Hiram said and Charlie helped him up to the vent Grille that opened up to let the Muses in and out. The two agreed to keep the secret. Ginge just gave a flat stare and then walked over to the warm inlet for the hot air heating system and curled up "He'll not give the game away... especially as there's spare Salmon on the go in the Canteen" Hiram dropped a hint. Getting the vent shut and settling back to his Pools Coupon Charlie waited for Derek to come in via the stairs

"You should have seen the chaos in the Arboretum... Somebody left the Skylights open; pigeons and other birds were all over the place. I made some quick sketches look" he said and handed Charlie his drawing pad

"I saw most of it on that old TV; it keeps picking up the CCTV cameras, though Lord knows how" Charlie said and looked at Derek's work. Considering how fast the sketches were done; individual details like the odd face you could recognise, the bird being grabbed at getting just out of reach; and the sights of the bemused Shoppers were like stills from an action movie with Motion blur. He'd captured the chaos of the event marvellously "We're doing the Works Newsletter This week... Get Delia to scan those in and we'll get them put into the composite. You can do it this time on your own. See how well you have learned it" Charlie said. Derek puffed up with pride. He; an apprentice was being allowed to composite a page or two alone... He was being honoured. Hiram suddenly felt relaxed as if a burden had been lifted. Skizzer looked in on his way to the Loading Bays. He had a few feathers sticking out of the claws of one paw. Hiram turned around and saw an ashen looking Gardenia

"He... Saw you and talked to you" she said as he explained the events she had obviously witnessed hidden from view

"...And he's fine with it. We have to keep the others out of the loop though. And he has seen you on the camera's... Says for a wee folk you have a fine body... he caught a glimpse of you on one of the security tapes bathing in the fountain I think. Relax; he destroyed the recording by recording a snooker match over it" Hiram said

"Oh I don't mind that he saw me naked... You could if you want. We Fays don't have those kinds of Hang ups; like most Humans seem to. Besides; I'm old enough not to care" she replied

"How old are you exactly; I'm pushing round seven hundred myself" he asked

"Older than you but not by much. I gave up counting the years long ago" She responded; and dropped a packet of Salmon she'd "acquired" from the Canteen, through the slightly open vent. It fell next to Ginge who opened one eye; then the other and meowed. Then looked pleadingly at the two Humans and pawed the packet. The smell of Salmon brought Skizzer in from the yard.

"That cat could smell food a mile away" Charlie said. He watched them both eat; and noted Ginge wink slightly.

The Discovery actually made things work better for Hiram and to a lesser extent for Gardenia. Tom was still getting writers block; and Gardenia reasoned that it must be the "Chi" of his workplace. So when he had left one night...

"Hamish; Hiram you move that desk a little more to the right. Whisper; that Mirror by the Washroom door, move it to the other side. I'll change the arrangement on this side board thing here. It will also help to tidy up the mess of cables from the printer; fax machine and Phone. It's a wonder that IT man doesn't hang himself he's so untidy" She said as they "rearranged" Tom's office layout. When they'd finished... Hiram had rigged a switch to kill the CCTV cameras. And the one on Tom's laptop was isolated by Hamish... who had learned a lot from watching one of the Tower Guard's nephews. There was a "software switch" that turned the camera off. A security feature. It also prevented a hijacker using it.... The place had a much tidier feel and "flowed" better. A note was left as if from the Cleaners to say they needed to move things to clean the carpet. And they all went to the Canteen.

The security Cameras in the Canteen had "developed issues" that afternoon. Gardenia found that putting Acupuncture needles in the cables would cause all sorts of wonderful effects. And confused the heck out of the Cable guys; when they were broken off, leaving the shorting bit still in the cable. The fault would persist till the cable was disturbed or replaced. Though trying it with one of the alarm cables had a really undesirable effect

"Ah hope the scunner gets the help from oor efforts the night" Hamish said

"I reckon he will be confused at the layout. But everything else is as he has it; just the furniture positions and the removal of some of those unnecessary decorations" Hiram said "But I can feel something different in him; a sort of lightness" he added

"I sense it too; and I got the items you wanted Gardenia"

Blox said as he arrived on Skizzer's back with a small bag. She took the bag and put the small pin like items in various places around the room. She had already placed the magnetic opposites of each pin in Tom's office at Chi Hotspots.

"That should do it; they will direct the Chi to him from all the collection points. He should end up supercharged" Gardenia said as they left "Sending the Charge of Chi to him here in the Canteen means we can concentrate on one area at a time. His writers block first I think" she added.

"I could do with a wash down. We hid in a dusty vent on the way over here" Blox said

"There's a new demonstrator shower in the Haberdashery department or the ones in the Director's Changing rooms" Hiram said. Gardenia laughed

"You could always bathe with me in the fountain in the arboretum" she said winking at Hiram who flashed Blue. The other Muses all looked a little shocked. She explained what Hiram had said as to what Charlie had done with the security recordings

"A Cardinal rule broken Hiram; and he's fine with it, how?" Whisper said and asked

"It seems; he's been aware of my helping for some time. And it could be hereditary. His Gran said all her life that she could see the little folk. I went to the Archive My Dad gave me before he moved on. And sure enough some Humans can sense us and other "unnaturals". However;

Blox decided in the end he'd use the Director's changing room's showers. Hiram found a set of his Dad's clothes for Blox to change into. They were a good fit; Blox being about the same size. Even the shoes. They all departed back to their own bases of operations; Gardenia making a detour to Bathe in the fountain, and give the Security recorders a section of noise to record by giving the cables the needle.

The Artist's rise

Guy Davis made an impromptu visit while Derek and Charlie were setting up the Monnan to do some of the Christmas cards from Derek's designs. Charlie had been teaching Derek how to engrave a plate. Using the photo etch system. Derek had become adept at doing the Stock Wedding invites and had made a new set of plates with a more modern look as a "Practical" project for his Apprentice work. He'd done such a good job Charlie had recommended the old plates be retired. He was riding a high when Guy dropped by

"I like the simplicity of the finished cards. Silk finish bond isn't it Charles?" he asked. He always used the formal address of Charlie's name.

"Yes Guy; and number three weight. The Monnan will do heavier; but this fits better in the envelopes. We print the template for those too. The girls in the Office like making them up. When they have a few spare moments. Or we can use stock C6" Charlie replied

"Derek you did these designs?" Guy quizzed

“Yes Mr Davis; and some other stuff. Oh Charlie the Bremman has finished the Works Newsletters. Our first edition in colour in years” he directed that to Guy. Davis took one of the papers and scanned through it and came across Derek’s action sketches

“Wow I haven’t seen that kind of style in oh… ten maybe twenty years. The young Artist who did this kind of work went missing on a trip to Nepal. Derek these are incredible. If ever you feel like you need an introduction to the Academy of Municipal Artists let me know? What are you like with caricatures?” he asked

“Haven’t thought of trying but Mr Hagan is sitting for a portrait; just to annoy the board instead of a Photographic portrait for the Directors Gallery” Derek said in reply

“Oh! That should be interesting to see. Charlie I hope you encouraging ...” he never got to finish As he spotted the Copper plate of a pastoral scene that Derek was reworking… Where did you get one of my Mentor’s plates from?” he said incredulously

“Oh that was here when the original presses were installed in here. We’ve cleaned and reworked some of the details over the years. It’s used for the Loose Chocolate Selection Boxes. Only One colour and the background of the stock. Hamptons have used it for all those years. Last year the colour changed to a dark green and that really showed off the original engravers shading technique brilliantly. But this year they are going for Crimson” Charlie replied

"He's still alive; he's a good age now, lives in a retirement home in Derby now I believe" Guy said "Can you do me a couple on Card?" he asked

"Will be a pleasure. And I'll give you one of the misprinted box prints on the right card. Go and get Denise in Confectionary to make it up for you; tell her I'll pay for the chocolates" Charlie said

"You'll do no such thing I'll pay. And Derek... keep this up and you'll be exhibiting in the Tate" he said and left with the Card prints and Two of the box misprints. Hiram watched this with interest. His Dad must have been here when that plate was first used. It would be just after that he met his Mum. He thought. He went to check the Archive of Memory glasses.

Gardenia was pleased with the results of the office makeover was having on Tom. He seemed inspired more and was taking Fluence more readily. He had the potential to be a top novelist... If he could afford the time to do the work in peace. The Workplace was distracting. But it was a trade-off she would need to bear. He'd had one of his short stories printed in the Local newspaper. It caused quite a reaction.... Mixed reviews always put some first timers off... But Tom seemed not to mind. He got word from the Board of Directors that he had the right now to take early retirement; or work limited hours till he felt ready to leave. His efforts in getting Hamptons "on the map" had earned him a lot of respect from the most influential of the board. And long term loyalty was always rewarded at Hamptons. Tom discussed the idea with his wife. Their two daughters were grown and had families of their own; so they had "Downsized" and had quite a nest egg from the sale of their old property. With the approval of the kids it was notable to add. So it wasn't as if they wouldn't be able to cope with him retiring early

"But you're such a stubborn bugger; you'd want to work till you drop. I know you only too well" His wife, Sybil, had said. Even Charlie agreed with her when he'd mentioned it.

"Limited hours then. And you can bet your last penny that Sybil will have me getting the cottage garden spic and span" he added chuckling "We got a bargain with that canal side place" he said

"She always could wrap you around her finger... it was her came up with the date of your wedding wasn't it?" Charlie said. He was right she had... easier for him to remember their Anniversary.

Blox's charge was moving on and he reckoned he'd done all he could anyway. They were on a roll and freewheeling now. And he was off to Manchester in search of new sparks. He'd keep in touch. The "Newbies" at the Canal paid a visit to Gardenia for some advice. There was a child was showing signs of the prodigy spark... something rare in one so young

"I had a few in my life; I'll need to scan them over. Is the Guest room still in the old drinking Fountain?" she asked him, she was distracted watching the play of the water in the fountain in the Arboretum

"Yes and it's been refurbished. Gone a little modern with those waterfall shower things. But it still has that hand carved bed" He said

“That had been a gift from a beau. He met with a nasty fate. It wouldn’t work here of course. I have a spare eiderdown for it though

“Oh we could do with that. The son came to visit to watch over a spark he’d found in the yachting fraternity. They were trying their hand a canal boats… Not the best of starts” he said… he was called Halyard Nivvor… She was called Hermione Graft originally. She drew herself away

“We only had the one child. I have a problem conceiving. My parents moved on before Halyard’s. They were Old School through and through” she said.

“Child prodigy’s tend to be very hard work. They have so much imagination it’s hard to balance them. But at least there’s two of you. There was only me with Albert… Mathematics mental that one” Gardenia said as Hiram dropped by on Ginge

“Have you seen Skizzer? He was supposed to be taking a message to that Bogeyman that runs the Chinese” Hiram said

“He’s been a bit distracted of late… I think it’s that female Tabby over at the Ice Rink” Ginge said

“You would; mind in the gutter. It’s end of season’s sale next week. He always comes back for that doesn’t he Hiram?” Gardenia responded

“Yes; won’t miss it. The treats he gets given… But he’s

never done anything like this. Even Charlie is finding it odd. When he does come around he's so tired he sleeps for hours" Ginge said. It was odd behaviour for the cat

"Skizzer that's the tabby with the white streak on his right hindquarter isn't it?" Halyard asked

"Yes; that's Skizzer. Birthmark from his mother" Ginge replied

"He's been hanging around the Canal Marina a lot lately. Since the Ferals were rounded up; the place is much more "friendlier" feeling" Hermione noted "he could be there" she offered. Hiram and Ginge went to check the place out

"Charlie's the Charge that knows all about us wee folk isn't he?" My uncle had one like that; a boy called George. Vivid imagination too. I have Uncle Fisticuff's memory Glass at home. You should check it out when you visit Gardenia" Halyard said... ...

Seasons

The end of season sale came and went and Skizzer did turn up... with a mate; the Tabby from the Marina. She was heavily pregnant. That explained a lot of his behaviour. She ended up settling in a box in the Stock Cupboard. Hiram had helped deliver kittens once before when he was a kid; so he did the Mummy watch. Floss was a young female and a little too young to have a first litter so there could be complications. Besides Gardenia was also available should he need her; a cats call away. Having Flossie at the store settled Skizzer and he soon became a "House Cat" for the Store. He earned his keep by keeping down the number of birds roosting in the eaves of the roof of the store and the rats that gathered around the Canteen waste bins; Ginge was good at Ratting too. So the store acquired two "unpaid" members to its staff. They were popular on that front too. And would often be seen wandering around the floors and were greeted with treats and "pettings" and "fussings" especially from the female staff. Charlie was now working with Hiram on Derek. Charlie from his apprenticeship front; Hiram from his artistic bent. The lad was really progressing in both areas fine. Derek was on a Day at college doing his Art Foundation Course and his final Apprenticeship qualifications. There was a new boy in the Mail Room who also looked promising for tutelage before "Charlie retired"

"... Funny thing is; Tom and me started together at Hamptons, and it looks like we'll both end up finishing together... Well full employment at least" Charlie said

"Yes; I heard from Gardenia about how Tom opted for the reduced hour's option and the late retirement. I also think it's great you're going to be a sort of Living Knowledge bank so to speak" Hiram responded giving Flossie a back rub in her lumbar regions

"Ooh! That's so much better Mr H. I've a feeling I'm going to be in labour a long time tonight. And Ginge is keeping that fussy mate of mine busy on night patrol thankfully" she said. Hiram didn't mind the moniker; he actually found it a bit more formal. Gardenia poked fun at it of course.

"That's OK Flossie. I've seen to many Birthing's in my time. And As Charlie will no doubt tell you; Fathers always are the worst worriers. It's a wonder any men survive without going totally insane with the fretting" he said chuckling. Flossie had a contraction spasm "That's a strong one... Not long now" he added

"I remember our Frankie's birth only too well. He was our second, Lydia was our first. He was such a determined one to get out he had poor Leona in a right state, me too" he said and he felt her pulse "Very strong; at least your heart won't give out. Is there any way to tell how many Hiram?" he asked

"Not really; a guestimate at best. From her size it's a good few, and there's a chance they'll be on the small side. So you will be feeding a lot" he said in reply.

Up in the Shop the last of the late-night Saturday shoppers were leaving and the security staff were seeing the management off. Charlie was getting ready to go up to the security room. He had another duty now as he was also taking reduced hours. He was night Caretaker at weekends. So the security got a break. Hiram went to his watch spot as they heard Corbin; one of the security lads come along the corridor with his distinctive clop of his boots

"Hi Charlie... Flossie; got a little treat from the girls in the canteen for the mum to be" and he uncovered a bowl with some fish heads from the filleting; Flossie perked up as the bowl was put in easy reach

"Our Candy was like Flossie here when we got her. Her first birth was a hard one on her. But this little 'un looks a lot fitter than Candy did. We are off now Charlie; we've got the new Camera's on the blink again. Somebody is coming in first thing Monday to sort out what's going on. I think it's the new-fangled equipment. The old fashioned video recorders gave less bother" Corbin said and left. After he and the others left. With the Days takings in the safety of the security van; to be deposited at the late night deposit point at the bank. He signalled for Hiram to come out and he headed up to the "Security Suite". He wasn't surprised to find Gardenia back and sat on the control desk

"You've been mucking about with the settings again haven't you" he said winking

"You know me too well Charlie. Oh; there's a bottle in the cupboard from Hamish. One of the Guards celebrated his Eightieth" she replied and panned the camera in the Arboretum to the fountain. There was an addition to the "Family" in the store, Gardenia had a Hubby... Blox.

"You're... Well he is your man. He knows you watch him does he?" and as if he'd heard he mooned the camera as he bathed. That made both of them laugh. "Our Frankie used to do that when he was a kid. Liked to show off; got all shy when he hit puberty though. Then when he was dating went all show off on the beach" Charlie said chuckling

"Me and the other Muses have been talking and we've reached a consensus. There is an honour a Muse can bestow on a Human that comes with great responsibility and it is given with great caution and care attached. There are enough of us to be able to do this honour... And the time is approaching fast if we do it this year. We can make you and Leona like us... You'd no longer age like you do;

and you'd have our powers. Joining the "Guild of the Wee Folk" is a great gift. You can refuse and nothing will come of it. But if you accept you will be bound by rules" she said while she watched Blox dry off and change. She'd found some scraps of moleskin in one of the Drawers in the haberdashery department and had made Blox a smoking jacket out of them. She had turned out to be an excellent seamstress

"I'm glad we could tell Leona what's going on here. She's been wonderful about it all. I take it you know that her Family are "Knowers" too" Charlie said rather than asked; as he had a suspicion as to the answer

"Yes; Hamish knew her great Grandmother as a child. The parents dismissed their daughters "seeing Fairies" as a thing she'd grow out of. But the gift had passed down the line. Maybe Frankie and Lydia will end up like you and Leona. Fate will tell in the end" she replied and they set themselves for the long night's work.

Tom finished yet another book while on a fishing trip to the Norfolk Broads. The "part-time" retirement was working out better than expected. Even Hagan was thinking along the same route; though keeping his Board attachments in an "Advisory" role. Tom seemed much more inspired lately. Since they'd done a rearranging of his "Writing Den" at home. He had even gotten used to his new Tablet computer and its touch screen; with its onscreen keyboard. And only being able to see a limited number of lines at a time. His grandson had come up with a better solution though and he was using that option on the trip. A Bluetooth keyboard with a trackball type mouse built in. He was getting so adept with it he almost left his electric Typewriter alone these days. He was a recognised author now. And the new apartments looking over the Marina development in by the Canal were perfect. The Cottage was set in trust for the kids initially.

Their neighbours below were paramedics; the ones to their right on their floor were Carers, so they had all the help an elderly couple could want on the doorstep. Regular visits from the family were catered for with the guest rooms. And they even enjoyed the grandkids popping in. Charlie and Derek had taken one of his first paperback novels and had created a "special" Leather bound Hardback edition for his Seventieth birthday. Printed on the Monnan with illustrations by Derek; it sat on the bookshelf in pride of place, and the grand kids loved to sit and read it and to admire the illustrations. Life was good; he did miss the store a little since fully retiring last month. But it was practically only a bus ride away. So he'd drop in once in a while. Visit Charlie and the gang. He even still had rights to the Company Outings. So his social life was also good. Gardenia had handed him over to Hermione. She had a second skill and had improved on Gardenia's inspiration. And they were close enough to the apartments and the Marina to cover the whole area. And the fountain in the Square of the Apartments development was a good replenishing point when needs be.

Gardenia and Blox worried that Hiram didn't have someone special in his life. So had sent out feelers through the birds. It was just before Christmas that a Robin dropped a note from a Muse in Newcastle-upon-Tyne. A female of the same kind as Hiram was "stranded" with no charges and was looking to move. They had worked in secret with the others to get her to come to the Town. Hiram had moved out of his home in the Monnan and was now resident permanently in the vents. He had rooms all over the place; and after some serious problems with the Crawler, the whole maintenance issues seemed to take care of themselves; and the thing was retired to the store cupboard… in the Basement. He still looked after the Machines… they were as much his charges as they were Charlie and Derek's. The gang had got together to perform the "Rite of Acceptance into The Guild" and the Full moon was to rise next Friday night. The Muse from the northeast had been living in secret with the Canal Family as the Water Fays were called these days. And out of sight of Hiram till the "Arrangements" for introducing her could be made. She had been secretly to the Store and shown around by Gardenia and Blox while Hiram had been out on a rare excursion with Ginge. Skizzer spent a lot of time with his family. Flossie had thirteen kittens in all. And they were a real handful. Couple of former Ferals turned up one day wearing Collars and name tags. They had been "adopted" by a family of Humans and they'd moved back into the redeveloped Canal area. They were fully domesticated now

"Just paying a visit to the old haunts. I don't even feel the same anymore; I even leave the pigeons alone… the Gulls are a different matter" one of them had said before they went to be "Housecats" again.

Glenda as the Muse was called didn't have a typical Geordie accent either. She had originally come from Oxford with her grandparents. They and her parents were "moved on" now and she was alone. She was an Engineering and technical Muse. So had fitted in well with the Student communities in Newcastle and Durham cities. But there had been a "drying up" of sparks for reasons unknown. Here she felt hundreds of potentials; and was driven to distraction by the possibilities. It had been decided to introduce Glenda at the Ceremony for the two elderly Humans. And she would more than make up the required number. The ceremony would take place at moonrise; around two hours from now. Glenda had been privy to one such ceremony before so knew what to expect.

Blox was at Charlie's house with Leona

"Will we become small like you?" she asked

"Oh no nothing like that; but you'd have all the powers though. You can become invisible if you need to. And I expect some others too that even we rarely use. You'll probably behave like kids with a new toy. That's what Glenda said the Gifted she'd seen the Ceremony performed on did. They were just like a couple of kids. But try and be sensible. Humans around you not accepted to know mustn't suspect. You won't live as long as we do; Human lifespan's can only be extended so much. But you will outlive the likes of Tom and Derek maybe. It depends how careful you are. The Ones that Glenda saw accepted decided to "fake their own deaths" and live off the grid so to speak. They never really got on well with their families so it worked out fine for them... you two will need to make your own arrangements on that front" Blox answered

"Glenda seems so wise for her age, she looks about thirty" Leona said

"She's about a hundred years older than Hiram, and he's not that much younger than me his older brother. We got separated when the rest of the Family moved on. I was over the moon when we finally found each other again. We reckon you'll both live at least two hundred or so years before coming to an end... "Moving On" as we call it. Not like any kind of death you could imagine. Just you fading away into another dimension and time. To be reborn and grow there all over again" Blox responded

"I'm sorry if I don't seem talkative today; I'm worried about Charlie. He's asleep now so best not disturb him The Weekend nights seem to get to him more these days" she said "I've noticed some changes in his body he seems not to have; and I don't know how to broach the subject" she added

"At his age Human men do have the chance of serious issues happening and they get embarrassed by it all. I'll have a word with him and find out if he's worried. If he is there's a simple solution. Get him down to the Doctors Clinic and have him get a "Human MOT" done. Put both your minds at rest. Personally I haven't seen anything to indicate anything very serious... he's probably just embarrassed about the changes that are happening. Old age even gets us eventually. And I dread going senile before I move on. That's what happened to my Uncle Glospire" He responded. He helped her find the number of Charlie's Doctor's and set up the appointment for Thursday.

Charlie was sleeping as she said that... he was having a small nightmare; the same one as it happened he'd been having for a while. It was after the ceremony and the two of them were about to try out their new powers... Leona was fine; but his were all over the place wrong. And he found parts of his body would disappear and others expand or contract when he should have just turned invisible. An attempt at sending inspiration into a Charge made the poor boy get horrible acne and made his parts swell. He just didn't seem to be able to get them to do what he wanted. The nightmare culminated with him shrinking to Pixie size and being snatched by a Gull which whisked him up into the skies only to plummet down when the Gull let go. He would inevitably then wake up because he had fallen out of bed. Gardenia had said that was only nervousness and it would pass. But he was worried. He had noticed some lumps forming in odd places around his body. And was worried he had cancer or something. He felt embarrassed when two lumps had turned up on his wotsit. He was trying to pluck up courage to talk with Leona about seeing the Doc.

Derek was not to know just yet; but Charlie had secretly had the Lad's Indentures formerly ratified and made up to present to him when the Store closed for the Seasonal Holidays. Hamptons never opened on Boxing Day; but the day after, a tradition that was handed down from founders. And New Year's too. More so if that fell on a Sunday; then there was no opening till a following Saturday. It was down to one of the Founders beliefs. And Christmas Eve fell on a Friday this year. So the store would be closed till Tuesday. He was to receive his Indentures at the close of business Christmas Eve; in time for the Company Party. And Old man Hagan came around with gifts for them all; dressed as Santa. That was two weeks away. When Flossie's kittens would be almost all weaned and could be made ready to go to homes. Three of the Toms had been earmarked for homes already. Five of the Girl kittens were on the hopefuls list. The rest were being groomed for local adoption by Board Directors families. So she was more relaxed. There had been no complications with the Birth and Skizzer was proving to be an excellent Dad... Sharing responsibilities; apart from feeding that is. And; courtesy of Ginge's contact The Bogeyman had a new message service. A couple of Ravens. He used them to send his cousin in Scotland news and views. And likewise he sent messages back. In return the building where the nasty Gulls were roosting had been "torched" one night before development fell into place. It looked like some local gang members had done it so he got a big windfall from the insurance company. Sold the shell to the developers who demolished it had built the second phase of the Apartments blocks on the substantial foundations.

All was falling in to place when the medical results happened the Thursday before the Full moon. The results of the tests came back. He had an elevated level of white blood cells... He was anaemic so would need iron in his diet. The lumps were just lymph infections and antibiotics should clear that up.... However there was signs in the blood that something may be up with the Testosterone production. This was having some other knock on effects to the other hormone levels in his body. It could explain some sleeping issues he was having. That meant a Prostate examination and the embarrassment that would cause. Also further tests to check out his thyroid function etc. And a battery of heart tests again afterwards. But they could be done after the New Year

"Just don't go overboard with the Drinking" had been the Doctors advice "Or if you do; have the Hospital's Urgent Care Number handy" was added as an afterthought

"Well love... It could have been worse" Leona said encouragingly

“We have to drink a special herbal potion for the ceremony… If it contains Valerian; then that will react with the Antibiotics according to the notes with these capsules… and I have to avoid taking them with milk or milky drinks” He said reading the prescription and advice notes “And Iron Sulphate tablets may turn your stools black” he added “Like they do when you have a cancerous bleed in the bowel. I’m not looking forward to that. At least it’s only for three months to pick me up.” He finished and looked at her

“Don’t worry; I’ll find out. You have to get some rest. There’s a board meeting for you tomorrow before we do the ceremony and if you’re nervous and tired from that you won’t be fit to have the powers flow into you” she said and made him go and rest.

When Gardenia heard about the Valerian and the milk avoidance she chuckled

“There’s no Valerian, though there is some Wormwood to it. As for the milk… Soy milk will help till he finishes the course. One of my younger charges had a tolerance issue with the Lactose in Cow and Goat milks. Moving to soy milk solved the problem… Till we got Lactose free Milk that is. So it should work for Charlie too. I know he likes plenty of milk in the coffee he drinks in the store. Just give it a good shake before using; especially in the coffee. Doesn’t make very good batter though” Gardenia responded

“Wormwood! … I can remember when I was a girl we used to get a tincture of Wormwood from our Chemists. It was for Colic in Babies and to help older children sleep…

Tasted ruddy vile though" Leona said in response; and they both laughed. Blox was out on patrol around the Gallery vents. Ginge said he could smell rats up there. So they were scouring the area to see if they were there and how they were getting in. "Rat urine carries a number of nasty diseases; some fatal. It depends upon their mental state or if they have some nerve damage if they spray mark. Normally a Rat is fastidious about keeping clean. More so than cats... Dogs are... well you know, you finally met Bowser" he said to Ginge

"Can't wash themselves and hate it when humans do it for them" Ginge responded and froze sniffing the air "Gordon from accounts is outside on the roof smoking that horrible herbal tobacco again" he added

"Well at least it's not the "illegal" sort. Had a charge once that was a total Pot head. Bong after bong all day sometimes. It's a wonder he had any working brain cells left" Blox said. And they were just about to go down a level when they spotted the opening. When the team had been investigating the Vents with the Crawler. They hadn't put the cover back on properly and the rats had bent back enough of the cover for them to gain entry. Blox had one of Hiram's spare tool kits and set to getting the gap closed and fastened so the rats couldn't get in or out. Gordon shuffled across to see what had made the noise and saw Ginge and shook his head and went back into the store extinguishing the hand rolled cigarette; and packing it away for later. He hadn't seen Blox as he'd ducked behind the vent housing out of sight. Ginge gave the all clear and they headed off again

"If there's one entrance in there has to be another or more... Right next sector " Blox said and they set off again.

The Friday evening was clear and crisp. There was nobody about at the rear yard of the shop. They were all gone now. Apart from Charlie; and Leona, the only others there were the Muses. The Cats were patrolling. The moon rise brought an eerie glow to everything. There was a frost forming and the reflected moonlight seemed to ripple and dart across the frosty surfaces as if it were a living thing. Hiram; Gardenia and Blox started the ritual by making the potion; chanting something in a language that the two Humans didn't recognise. Whisper and the others that Charlie knew were chanting a sort of counter verse. Hiram offered the Couple the strong smelling potion and they took a swig each. Hamish had spiked it with some fairly decent Scotch to kill the other tastes. It began to work almost immediately. The chanting started again and the Muses joined hands and started to glow. The Fays glowed greenish white; the others blue. The powers they were transferring began to make the air glow in streamers reaching out and towards the couple. They felt a strange tingling as the tendrils of eerie lights touched various parts of their bodies, and then Hiram spoke in English

"To these Charges we give our Blessing; our spirits and our powers. Entrusted through a bond of faith ancient and true" then there was a kind of lightning dancing from the reflected moonlight and the couple felt themselves lighten and begin to rise. The Gathered Muses reached a chorus of voices

"To the faith everlasting; to the life long and pure, to the world's heart and wisdom we give all to thee. There was a clap of thunderous like sound and everything that was glowing went out. Only the moonlight; the night's stillness and the shadows cast by the full moon were left. The muses approached the couple and each touched them in turn. And then the rite was over

"It will take a time to begin to show" said Hiram; but you will know when the powers are ready. I almost forgot the last line which we Muses have to say in our minds. But you are like us now. You will see the sparks; and feel the effect it has to give inspiration. It's almost like a kind of love; but there's something else there behind it. I can't put it into words; but you'll know it when you feel it. And don't be too surprised you can hear and speak with the animals... It's part of being a Muse. With the knowledge of the years you two have; any charges you take one will no doubt turn out right." Hiram said as they all went to the Basement. While the others were out, the New Muse Glenda had been busy. She had put together a spread of foods for both the Humans and the Muses and had moved into the Shadows out of view

"When did ye dee this?" Hamish said to Whisper

"It wisnae me" she replied

"Nor any of us either Hiram... There's someone here come from the North to be with us; Glenda show yourself girlie" Gardenia said. Glenda stepped out of the shadows and walked up to Hiram; she equalled him in height, was as blue as him, but had blonde silky hair down to the waist. She looked to be younger than Gardenia, but Charlie knew now that meant nothing when it came to telling the age of a Sprite. She wore a slim pale red dress suit

“I am here for you to help in what ways I can. I am here to serve in love and kind. I will obey all you command me to. If I dissatisfy you may cast me aside as is the old right” she said flawlessly

Hiram went bright blue

“Well answer her you daft gowk” Blox said

“I accept your offers with my heart and trust; I offer my self to your embrace. I give no token; of binding in haste. I shall make that by my hand and grace. I have to you as you have to me; the right given over for all to see. Take me in hand bound; to have and to hold till the moving beyond gets us in its grasp” Hiram responded with tears running down his cheeks. He remembered the words he had seen his other brother say to his life companion.

“What just happened?” Leona said

“Och! Twas jist a Muse wedding that’s all” Hamish said. Charlie almost choked on a mouthful of a steak sandwich

“When did this get planned?” He said just as puzzled as Leona and the other Male Muses.

“I asked Glenda to come down and watch over Hiram as I saw the “Loneliness” creeping up on him that got Uncle Grumman. A Muse at his time of life should never be alone” Blox said and raised a glass

“To ye both. Live long; love strong and be together all the times you can” he said and the other Muses repeated the toast. Hiram kissed Glenda long and hard. Now it was her eyes that ran tears… tears of love and joy. They feasted well. Looking down from the air vent Skizzer and Flossie nodded

“When that Gull said that there was a lone Muse in the City up North, I told Blox. He went missing that week remember. He was up there enticing Glenda to come here. That was when you found me hurting from that rat bite. And you cared for me. Watched over me and defended me. If that Bogeyman hadn’t come along when he did…I owe so many so much. But the only reward I wanted you gave me. The last five we reckon should go to the Directors…” Skizzer said

“Hush; you’ll wake them all. To be truthful; I was frightened all the time. Till you took on that rat. And getting me here to birth was a stroke of genius. You may not have sired those kittens asleep in that drawer; but you’ll be more of a father than the bastard that caught me. He was the one eyed Tom, the Grey Silky, Leader if the Ferals once till he was bested. That’s how he lost the eye. Frag they called him. I ran away when I fell pregnant and he followed me. How I made it through the busy traffic I will never know. He didn’t make it and was crushed under the wheels of a lorry. An evil hearted bastard gone and good riddance” Flossie said

“Oh there’s still time for us both to have our own litter together. But for now… Let’s just watch them sleep” Skizzer said and they worked their way back down to the Stock Cupboard.

Derek Indentured and something strange at the Works party

It was the end of work for the Season. Christmas Eve Shopping over the Store closed and the Staff gathered. The Canteen had been decorated and laid out for the Annual party. The store had only opened till noon. And it was made clear that shoppers would have to leave early. Hiram and Glenda were the only Muses present at the "Handing out" ceremony. The usual company gifts; the special awards... Ginny from Lingerie had rung up a record sales total beating the existing record by a good margin. The Team in Haberdashery got a special award for their efforts in the demonstrations they had put on. ... Then came the Apprenticeships awards. Simon got his first... he was actually shocked to find he was given not only full indenture; but a key to the executive washrooms. . There were some others from Accounts and Sales; Inventory etc. Then it was Derek's turn. Charlie had turned up on stage to present the Indentures to Derek with Hagan and Tom. It was the way Charlie was dressed that got a collective gasp from the others in the room. He was wearing the Historic Uniform that the Print Workers used to wear. Complete with the black Breeches and the flannel cravat. He wore the silk gloves of a Master Compositor. And the waistcoat of the Master Printer. Derek wore his best suit for the occasion. He was asked to get down on one knee. He hadn't expected any of this

"I have the great honour; to present my Apprentice... Nay my former apprentice. Now to be a Full and indentured Master Printer; to hold the office for as long as he can. And to carry with it the office of Print Room Master of all" Charlie said the oath he'd had said over his head when he'd been indentured. He held the indentures above

Derek and made a pass from right to left" Stand Full Master and take the words" he said and handed Derek the leather bound folder containing his indenture Documents.. He whispered as he bowed in front of Derek "You must break the seal and show the Management the indentures as proof. Then a short bow and step back" Derek did as instructed. He was astonished to see the documents and the embossed gold seal of the Presenting Agency. The Copper plates for each of the folded pages were also in the folder, which explained the weight. He turned the Open Folder to Tom and Hagan and they nodded approval. They took the folder and resealed it and shook his hand and handed the folder back

"Go out among your fellows with pride. And to all here be it known... Derek not only completed his Apprenticeship; there is a second presentation to give him... Mr Davis would you do the honours.

Guy Davis took the stage and had a large envelope with him. Two of the Mail room boys brought on three easels on the stage and set them up

"I have here the approval documents from the Tate Exhibition Committee for two of your works to be placed in exhibition in the Gallery in London in an exhibition of new talent reflecting everyday life. The works chosen reflect the range and skill of your art. He handed the envelope to Derek and the boys brought out the Sketches, now mounted and framed and set them on the easel. One was the Scene of the Arboretum from the Gallery. The other was one of the "action" sketches "Space was limited and the Committee would like you to accept their apologies that more of your work could not be shown... However there is still a slot for a collection to be displayed in the January calendar. I have asked they keep it free for you" Guy said and shook Derek's Hand "Now Mr Hagan; Derek has something for you and the Directors" he said and stepped back as the third; concealed work. Derek was blushing as he revealed the Portrait he'd done in pencil of Mr Hagan for the Directors gallery. Two of the directors who had Joined Hagan on the stage gasped... and the eldest among them spoke

"Boy; I don't know how; but not only have you captured Hagan so perfectly, you have shown a hint of his ancestral line. Mail Boy Go to My office and bring the Sketch from the Wall behind my desk" he instructed. There was a wait as the boy did as instructed and a fourth easel was set up. Beside the picture of Hagan the boy returned and placed the framed sketch on the easel.

"Your Great Grandfather was one of the Founders of Hamptons. He never wanted his image to grace the gallery while he still lived. Look now Hagan and see where you came from and from this day forth I say that both portraits shall hang side by side. What say my fellows?" He addressed that to the other directors. As one the all said "Aye; be it so". Derek was feeling faint. The signature on the Founders portrait was that of his Grandfather. In the vent watching the proceedings Hiram glowed bright and Glenda had to hold him down he was rising into the air. Blox and Gardenia were behind him

"I thought I recognised that spark... I was his Grandfathers Muse" Blox said "I was just turned puberty when Dad handed him to me. Saying "Work with this one; mould him and help him. He will be an artist one day"... he was right of course. Derek's Grandfather was Jason Jarman

Hilkes. The War artist that captured the aftermath of the Somme in his sketches for the Times. He worked from the early Tin plate and Daguerreotypes; that the reporters sent from the front to make the illustrations, as it wasn't possible at that time to print a photograph clearly in grey scale in the newspaper" he continued

"Derek looks nothing like his Grandfather though; I met the man by accident. I was influencing a Dancer at that time." Gardenia said. Hiram managed to calm himself and settle back down and stop glowing.

"Your Father would be proud of you both right now I would imagine... Among my family it was said that when a living Muse did beyond the fore; the ripples bounce through time and space to those that have "Moved On". All your ancestors probably know by now from the way you were beaming" Glenda said
Charlie at the back of the stage thought a message to the vent opposite

"I suddenly feel something I don't understand. And I sense that Leona does too. It's as if we are all being watched. I hope you get this as I can't leave the stage just yet. I will come back to the basement to change we can talk then I suppose. By then Leona will be joining us for the party" he finished

"Well the powers seem to be cutting in. and He's sensing the same as I do" Gardenia said; "that will be from me. He's right it's as if we are being watched... And it's not menacing either. I just can't fix where it's coming from" she added

Hiram tried his ability to scan for fluence at work "Found it... Oh; it's down by the Canal area. The new apartment block. They are reading our minds and thoughts. They are very young though?" he said puzzled

"And I sense it's not exactly Sprite or Human... Very odd" Gardenia said "I'm getting it now" Glenda said "I ... Yes! I know what it is. When I was staying with Halyard and Hermione; I slept in that Bed you left there Gardenia. I found a dried out Sogor Seed. I threw it into the ash from the fire that burned the warehouse down that stood there. It must have been blown to another part of that site and germinated" She added

"Sogor Seed?" Hiram asked

"It's an intelligent species of plant. Things turn up from time to time from across the dimensional divides. My Great Uncle Harvey Glost had one that he came across. They are acutely sensitive to the minds of animals. They have to be they are tasty to the right creatures. It must have become aware. The conditions have to be just right for it to germinate. If it's as young as Hiram sensed; then it will not yet be mobile. We need to track it down. Its mental influence could cause no end of chaos for the Humans hereabouts. That young and mobile they tend to have a mischievous side" Gardenia answered. Hiram sent a thought message to Charlie to bring him up to speed. He was in the Basement changing into his party clothes. Hagan had foregone the Santa suit this year and Charlie was doing the honours. It was either him or Gordon from accounts... Admittedly he had the better figure for the role; so Charlie was wearing pillows from the Bedding section of the Haberdashery floor to fill out the suit. He was going to get hot and sweaty; but he wouldn't disappoint. He thanked Hiram for letting him know and when Leona arrived he took her aside and let her in on the discovery

"You know Charlie... You suit that outfit. Why not do the Store Santa next year. You as Santa me as a Helper. We can check out the kiddies for sparks for the others; or take charges ourselves" She said later when the Santa role was over. He'd taken out the padding and the suit now hung comfortably loose

"That sounds a brilliant idea and you are doing the Schools Living History circuit; as I am... We can help the Muses no end. I knew there was something I married you for... Inspiration" he said and she jokingly punched him. The drink was having an effect already

"That must be another side effect of the Powers" Charlie said. Derek came over

"Finding my Granddad's work here in the store was a revelation. The only piece left that the family have is a watercolour of the Norfolk Broads he did before he died. Old Man Hagan and Guy Davis are looking to Have the Haberdashery department hold a display of his works in front of the Muses Artwork" he said

"Good for you. And promise me... When you take charge of the Print Room... Leave something for the Pixies to do" Charlie said seriously enough for Derek to question whether or not Charlie *was* being serious or joking.

Ginge and Hamish went along one side of the site, Skizzer and Halyard the other. It was Halyard found the young plant

"It's over here by the spoil heap. Have you brought that Pot?" Halyard asked Hamish

"Aye, and the Compost tae" Hamish replied. Working quickly they transferred the plant to the pot; and using a small Drag along cart from the Toy Department managed to trundle the Cart and plant to the Canal couples domain. It was a disused railway workers hut that had been left in place to "Add Character" to a scenic part of the Canal walk, it was in the sensing range of the Apartment blocks and other developments and there was always the Marina site accessed by a disused Sewer pipe. They had a section of frosted Glass bricks set into the ceiling in the area below a rear to the Maintenance shed for the Marina. The plant would be fine there for now.

"What are we going to do with it? It will be mobile soon and we will have all sorts of problems keeping up with it" Hermione said

"I vaguely remember a ritual to open a Gateway to the world they come from... But as I said vaguely. I was very young myself when my Parents performed the ritual to send another grown plant back" Halyard said

"The Rite of Removal or Hargoth Ya?" Hamish said

"Yes that's it" Halyard replied

“I ken’s it. And I ken where we can get the requirements tae” he added to his first statement.

The Print Room was ready to take its new Master; the other sprites and Fays had it gleaming. One day Charlie would let Derek in on the secret of the Print Room carers. Flossie had the kittens weaned now and they were boisterous. She let them explore from time to time. Some were ready to be homed now; but two of the Boys were showing signs of getting vicious. Skizzer took them aside and gave them a dressing down

“If you go Feral, you will end up in the Canal or in the Custody of The Animal Catchers” he said. He’d taken them to the Bogeyman at the Chinese takeaway

“And if you don’t wise up you might end up in one of my curries… or a Stir Fry” He said threateningly. That did the trick. Flossie called it cruel and unusual punishment; but she had to admit it was effective.

Derek would have Charlie to help for a while. And there would be the assistance of two of the new General Store assistants when he needed them. Till he got his own apprentice to train. Things seemed to be going well and the powers came in gradually. The couple saw their Sadie and Robby more and doted on the kids. Tom; now moved to Surrey had sent each of the Kids a set of his books. And the illustrated edition of his Children’s fairy tales. It was a best seller. And it brought Commissions for Derek. He followed Charlie’s advice about always leaving some work for the Pixies to do. And it was always done. And the logs completed. A New addition to the Basement machines came with an old Linotype copier. It needed a lot of attention. Charlie had used these pre-photo copier devices in his early days of being at Hamptons. To make copies of Sales and invoices etc. He always seemed to end up with more of the oily, waxy ink on his overall than in the machine. It had been found in an attic space above the Canteen when a new set of cabling for Free Internet terminals for the public was fitted. Charlie couldn't remember who'd had it put up there or why.... None of the older lot at Hamptons could either. It was a mystery; and even Hiram didn't and he'd been at the site far longer.

"The "Thing", the crawler, was "brought out of retirement" by the Muses and used to get about to area's not served by the Pneumatic Pipes. It was even loaned to Hamish and Whisper at the Tower. They'd come across a series of hollow channels in some of the walls just the right size to send it down. Why they had been put in place when the castle was built was another mystery. But they were ideal to get between some levels. And the Moat area outside.

The rite went perfectly and the mobile little plant shot away through the Gateway and to others of its kind. A Message of thanks was sent as the Gateway shut. Things were beginning to go as peacefully as they could... till one day about a Month from Blox's Birthday... a strange sensation hit all of them; even Charlie, Leona and the Cats. It felt like a supernatural or an Unnatural presence. But didn't seem to have a focus. And it seemed to home in on Derek. Hiram had vacated the Monnan for a more advantageous home overlooking the whole Basement. And he and Glenda would never be disturbed or heard for that matter

"Phew, what's that awful stink?" she said"

It's the presence; it's coming from one spot I think. But what I'm sensing otherwise is from everywhere but that spot. Like a poltergeist torn apart. It doesn't seem malevolent though; just exceedingly ancient and vague" Hiram said. Charlie sniffed the air

"Derek; have the Maintenance crew check the sewers and the drains. I think we have a leak. ... On second thoughts; continue with that order for the Sports floor.... I'll go and find Fred. He should be in the Men's Public Washrooms" he said and left. He thought to Hiram

"That smells stale and old. Almost like an old bookstore at the height of a humid summer" he thought

"Come to the Arboretum; I think Gardenia has a possible answer, or rather Whisper does" Blox thought back. He found Fred and told him about the reek and then headed to a Staff corridor that was little used. Gardenia and Whisper were waiting with Ginge who they were giving instructions to

"Right tell him Whisper" Gardenia said

"I think we have an old Sprite version of a Bogeyman, but I can't be certain. They are basically the thoughts and memories of a Bogey that had "Moved on" with unfinished business. They; or rather their memories, get stuck and left behind. Only another Bogeyman can rid the poor thing of its condition" She said

"Oh so Ginge is going for the one that runs that Chinese takeaway... He's a bloody good chef; I'll say that for him"

Charlie responded

“We had one here before the war once. From what Blox here says” Gardenia said

“Yes” Blox said arriving. It was when old Hagan’s Grandfather ran the business just before the War. It came through just like this one; seems to follow some old Ley line” He said “That one was dealt with by a Family of Bogeys that Lived near the Park back then. That was decimated when the German Bombs went off course. They moved temporarily into the sewers below the Store. It may be sensing an old trace of them” he added
‘It don’t half reek” I can’t understand why nobody else smells it much” Charlie said. Gardenia laughed

“That’s because now you’re one of us; your senses are heightened. Smell; taste, hearing... All of them” she said. Charlie felt a little foolish for not realising. He was getting a text message from Leona “Oh rats! The Cousins from Australia have just called; they are arriving in a couple of Hours. They have somewhere to stay while they’re back in Blighty, but need one night” Charlie said and looked glum

“Cousins?” Blox said quizzically

“Bert and Freda Willkiss. They were relations from my Mum’s side. Emigrated years back. I didn’t think they were still alive” Charlie said “They always tend to rub Leona up the wrong way. We were going to have the Grandkids stop over. But that’s out of the question now” he seemed to be panicking. Hiram ran a little fluence over him to calm him as he arrived.

“Glenda is watching a couple of promising hits among the school party looking at the Art show and the Muses Artwork. The girl is really strong. Thinks a little too logically though… the boy is good to better than average, but could be worked with” he said

“Leona is going to need some fluence to cope with Bert and Freda while I’m doing the School visit” Charlie said still distracted by the news “isn’t there some kind of thing we could do to them to say Freeze them till the following day or something else like that?” He asked

“Sorry; but we’re not allowed, after the incident that resulted in the Mongolian horde rampaging around. That Sprite got exiled to the Dungeon Dimensions for that influencing. Not every influence goes right; and hers went very wrong” Hiram answered “Dad told us the story; remember Blox?” he directed the question at his older brother

“Indeed I do. Had Sis frightened for three months with her charge… he was a physicist working here in England for the Americans in the Nevada Desert during the Second World War. Our family left and separated after that. And Mum and Dad “Moved on”” he said. Charlie began to understand the responsibility that goes along with being a Muse and; oddly, didn’t regret it, nor, he could sense, did Leona.

The relatives visit was short lived. It turned out they were “doing the rounds” one last time. Their health was fading now and they decided to drop the globetrotting and settle in Woomera in Northern Australia. They had picked out a nice place; Leona felt a little envious if truth be told, and were going to just keep in touch by the internet with their kids and their families

“We seem to be the last of Your Mums line Charlie. All the others have stepped over the great divide” Bert said

“When you get to our Age group you do tend to find that. We’re about thirteen years apart... You two must have been awfully young when you got married” Leona said to Freda

“Aye; Fred was stationed in the Army Training Corp in Glasgow at the time we fell for each other. How could I let such a marvellous specimen go without a decent woman tae guide him? Besides; it was a guid way to keep warm in the Bomb Shelters. He was only just a Civvie. But working for the Ministry was a fine opportunity tho’” Freda said, her Glasgow accent softened with the Brisbane twang she’d developed living in Australia. They stopped; as they’d said they would, just the one night, but as Freda was leaving she gave Leona an envelope with the instruction to open it when she got the word” Leona was tempted to read her mind; but gave that up, willing to find out the mystery as it happened. The Bogeyman was quick to perform the rite and the wandering Bogey Sprite got the ticket to Oblivion... That is a suburb of a domain; most nonhuman beings end up. It still took a couple of weeks for the reek to fade though. The downstairs Ladies Facilities for the staff was where it had settled strongest. The Bogey Sprite had been female in life so it seemed a natural place to perform the rite

“I have only ever done that procedure twice before... A wanderer; as we call them is a rare occurrence. But if left can fester and destroy a place. It seems cruel; but it is the best move after all. And it's not as if Oblivion is a gloomy place… it's a bit like the leafy suburbs of Wiltshire. My Dad opened a portal there once so we could see where he intended to retire" the Bogeyman, called George Chang, said.

Days seemed to go quickly; and Tom was next to be trouble; Derek had a dual career after Charlie finally retired fully. Tom was having difficulty with a new novel… An Adult fantasy work

"I just don't know how I go on from this point he said to his daughter Valerie. His wife had passed away unexpectedly from a brief illness. The Autopsy revealed she'd had a tumour that had gone unnoticed and poisons from that had almost destroyed the adrenal gland functions. She had too little strength in the end to combat the pneumonia. It had led to Tom being morose and writing a very dark tale; a Children's horror story. This was an attempt at brightening the mood. But it didn't seem to be working. Charlie and Leona paid him a visit. He was brightened immediately when they arrived on his Doorstep. He'd moved to The Norfolk Broads permanently; had a lock Masters Cottage on a Canal near to a mooring spot where there was a village Pub.

"I see you have all the amenities handy" Charlie said

"Oh the pub! Yes; Valerie is my youngest and stays with me here. While She studies in Norfolk. Val, come and say hello to my old friends… He hasn't seen you since you were a toddler" Tom said

"Val, the toffee thief… My oh my!" Leona said

"Aunty Leona, Uncle Charlie... Wow but you two look great. Dad's always reminding me I should pay you two a visit now and again" the young woman said as she came in from putting the car in the garage at the rear of the property "I was going to drop by on my way up to Carlisle. I have a boyfriend who's moved up there into his parent's old place; stuck in a time warp that old building. Says he needs inspiration in decorating it" she added. As the four chatted the elderly couple "did the biz" as they called the fluence treatment.

Tom's mind was a mess of conflicting emotions and thoughts. It took the two of them working alternately to sort out his head. And drop the inspiration in. In the end Tom thought he'd come up with the idea himself... which is what any good Muse wants as an outcome. Whether it was because they both knew the charge personally or not; was never decided upon. But the "kick-start" had Tom almost too fired up. In the end he did the work based upon his experiences as he had hit puberty and onwards. It had Best Seller written all over it. Even Valerie; who proof read her Dad's work, was shocked by some of the depicted scenes

"Did you really do that?" or "I would never have thought that of you Dad" were common comments; but she actually enjoyed the experience of reading, what was basically a confession of her Father's youth "I've highlighted the typos and the suspect punctuation... but Dad, that's really hot stuff. Tell me any Adult publisher who'd turn down that work and I'll show you a Victorian Prude. Dad it has the feel of a modern work. I'm proud of you" and she hugged and kissed him. He went through the corrections and used his electric typewriter to create the corrected Draught Copy for the publishers in New York. It would cost a bit to send air Mail; but could be worthwhile. He also corrected the work in the Word processor package and printed out some more copies to send to a number of publishers

"The first to come back without any alterations they want doing we go with right?" Tom said to his Daughter after Charlie and Leona had left

"Too true. They'd only water it down... I reckon it could be Price Waterhouse" or that American one based in New York, they're always controversial. Always in the best sellers list though" Valerie replied. On the Train back the couple smiled knowingly at the result of their work

"Now; Hiram said there was that boy among the school kids, you and her Mum are in the WI, you do him. I'll concentrate on ... Horace Webby... Post Office Clerk with the potential to be a brilliant Engineer if he'd just get the backbone" Charlie said

"Oh I know who you mean... Bossy woman. It's probably down to her he's so reluctant to get independent. Wants him to take after his older brother and get a University degree... Horrible kind of person that does that to a kid" Leona said. They had made up their minds and thought messaged to the rest. Glenda got Leona's impression of the woman and had laughed a little loudly while they had watched the Lunch crowds in the Canteen and had elicited "looks". Hiram scowled at her but also laughed

"I know the kind too" he thought back "Never amount to much themselves though... And usually when they do they end up making things bad for everyone else. That Thatcher Woman; she should have been fluenced to give up Politics and stick to Greengrocery" Hiram added.

A New Generation arrives

Two years had passed since Glenda had come into Hiram's life. And he was surprised one afternoon after coming back from a patrol with Ginge. Skizzer was with the Canal Fays with Flossie being taught the same duties that he had. He was aligned with Hamish and Whisper in London. He'd found out how to get free rides on the trains. She was weeping and smiling. Confused he approached her

"What's up love?" he asked expecting something bad.

"Oh; just my emotions up set... nothing to fret about... Tis only a woman's thing. It's a pity that Blox and Gardena are up in Glasgow to sort a Charge out there who moved away from Town. I've sent a message via crow to Gardenia about it" she said, sniffed and dried her eyes

"Is there anything I could do?" He asked. That elicited a glare he immediately backed away from. He decided to leave the subject be. He'd seen that look in a female Human once and it was clear that the man should back away. It's a common enough gesture and look among all females of all species. Except maybe Spiders and other arachnids; who had other designs on their mates when the deed was done.

They were kept Busy with Derek and his apprentice of late. Derek was getting more Commissions for illustrations for Author's book covers. He was getting very adept at it and it fitted in with his Duties in the Print room. Guy Davis became a regular visitor and he brought his Daughter with him from time to time

"Young love's going to flourish there" Glenda had said... She wasn't wrong either. She became a regular visitor. Much to the Annoyance of "Young" Charles; Derek's Apprentice. He was every bit as green as he'd been when he started, but was learning fast. It was he who had found the remains of Hiram's Press hide out one day when he'd needed to change a fuse in the Monnan

"This looks like the old Dolls furniture in the Archive display in the Toy Department... you know the Fifties range" he'd said. Hiram had breathed a sigh of relief when the lad had left it at that. Charlie and Leona visited less often; but still made an effort to. It would soon be time for the couple to make plans for their "Deaths". Before that could happen they needed to be taught a few "tricks of the trade" since their powers were now fully in situ. One skill they may need to master Leona was looking forward to immensely... Invisibility. Another; Telekinesis, was what Charlie wanted to master. He had something in mind for that. So for the next week or so the respective Muses helped the couple master the skills. The rest might come naturally that would have to be seen.

Instead of sending a message; Gardenia showed up at the store and immediately took Glenda aside from the others. Giving that same look that said "No Men Allowed". Ginge sniffed the air

"I have an idea what's going on; but it's not my place to say" was all he would say. Glenda had been spending a lot of time in the Couples newly made Bathroom part of their Home. More so in the mornings. She had also been gaining a little weight; or so Hiram thought. He wasn't sure; as she had taken to wearing very loose clothes. Even Leona was giving nothing away yet. From what Charlie could sense in his wife. It seemed the Menfolk would have to stay none the wiser for now. Though something in the back of Charlie's mind recognised the signs and three days later it hit him... Hiram was going to be in for a shock. The kind of shock that stays with you for the rest of your life. He allowed himself a wry smile and thought guardedly "Do Muses smoke Cigars?" The Telekinesis training went better than the invisibility. But with practice the couple soon had both perfected. And had also worked out how their "Demise" would go. Ostensibly they were going to go and Visit Bert and Freda and some incident would befall the couple and they would be lost in the outback. The Muses had taught them a trick that meant the surviving relations wouldn't question the fact their bodies had not turned up. "Probably eaten by Gators" would be the presumption. When all they were going to do was use another skill; that of The Charm or The Glamour. To change what people saw of them and their faces.

"It has to be done from time to time; or you'd end up having to spend the rest of your lives invisible" Halyard had said. Leona said that might actually be fun... Charlie wasn't so sure.

Hiram had noticed his wife Glenda was putting on an awful lot of weight; and did seem to be eating a lot more than usual.... But it still didn't register what was actually going on. She was almost twice her size around the waist now and the loose clothes were starting to become tighter. He'd admonished her one day about getting too fat. She had actually laughed at him and said he'd see? That was a right puzzle and no mistake. Charlie; when he and Leona had an alone moment had actually come out with what he was thinking

"She's pregnant isn't she... Glenda... She's with child" he said

"You've guessed then... OK but don't let on to Hiram or the other Muse Menfolk... they'd only cause a fuss. All the Women know; including Flossie, her Kittens are doing fine in their new homes. But with Muses; there's a twist to pregnancy Humans and other creatures don't have. As she and Hiram are Sprite Muses... Then there's a little complication that could be hazardous if not handled with care" Leona explained what Gardenia and Whisper had said. She told him as they had told it to her.

"Well; that does complicate things... And she has to be alone all the time... it's a bit like the Indian Squaws. When they give birth they are to do it alone; and if that bleeding happens when Glenda gives birth... Hiram isn't capable of coping on his own" Charlie said worried now

"Oh; she won't die from it... It just means she can't have any more" Leona said. If the Bleed doesn't happen... then there could be another in a few years" his wife added. So Hiram and the others were kept in the dark. From what Leona was told. Glenda's waters would break around the next full moon and High tide. The Wee Folk did a lot of things according to the phases of the Moon; including give birth it seemed.

Charlie and Leona Tried out The Glamour on the people they thought would possibly recognise them after they were "Dead". It worked like its other name said... A

Charm. It even worked on the Cats and Bowser. He sniffed the strange old couple... To him they smelled just as an old couple should smell. Everyone they tried it on fell for the disguise. Sadie and the Grandkids had been the funniest; they thought they'd given the game away when Sadie said

"You remind me so much of my Parents; they do so many of the same things... its uncanny"... Flossie was another surprise. She seemed to see through; or rather partially through Leona's Glamour. But couldn't put a paw on what was not right. Hamish had sensed her confusion; and had calmed it before Whisper could object. Everything looked to be ready and the time to do it was fast approaching. Glenda and Leona were alone together a day before the couple would have to leave for the flight to Australia.

"We're going to miss your event... It's a real shame" Leona said

"I've thought about that and have the "Thing" set up where I will birth to record it for you and Charlie... I hope he's not squeamish" Glenda said

"Charlie! Squeamish... he was there all through Sadie's birth even wanted to help the Doctor out" Leona said laughing "There'll be no problems there lass. Just you come through this intact for us; that's all we need from you. And let us help with the Naming please" Leona replied and asked

"Of Course. If it's a Boy Hiram has say; that's Sprite tradition, but a girl... that's for all of us. Girls are special and have a respect boys don't have" Glenda had said.

Hamish and Whisper were going to be the ones to see the couple get their flight and away. They had taken one of Flossie's Kittens for the Tower Guard to find. They had adopted the girl kitten immediately. They had named her Freesia after the flower box she'd turned up in and her free spirited look. As the elderly couple's plane took to the Skies they left to go back to the Tower.

The couple enjoyed the flight; checking for Sparks and noting them for future reference. Charlie enjoyed the inflight meals and drinks a little too much... But one of the Benefits of their new existence was how quick the effects of overeating and alcohol left the body. They made sure everyone noticed them on board and would remember how nice a couple they seemed to have been. "So jolly and full of life" one of the passengers would say when their deaths were announced. They even dropped in on Bert and Freda briefly; in Glamour of course. Before they found a plane heading back. Being invisible helped and the flight had two spare seats for passengers that had mysteriously not turned up in time and the flight had departed without them. So they had seats for all the flight. Meals and drinks were taken care of by surreptitious telekinesis. And hiding away to avoid being seen. Walking clean through Customs invisible was a hoot. The Security lads on the Scanners were totally bamboozled as to why they went off when there was nobody there. That was down to the Change in Charlie's pockets and Leona's necklace and bracelet. They sent a thought message to say they were back and they would be taking the train up to the town.

As it happened all that had only taken five days in total. And; due to some mistiming on Glenda's body clock. They hadn't missed the birth. But the jig was up when ...

"Oof! Hiram give me a hand up please" Glenda said as they got ready to do a round of the Print Room machines. Glenda had kept working as normal during her pregnancy letting the jokes about her size and weight slide. It was beginning to feel like she was carrying twins. Hiram helped his wife up and she got on the back of the modified Toy Truck they were now using to get along the corridors. A pump had failed on the Pneumatic system and a new one was on its way from Connecticut... they were only one of two suppliers of this equipment and they were based there... the other in China; and they would have to make one with the right voltage adjustment since most of their parts went to Asia and Seoul in South Korea. That pump was due to arrive tomorrow special delivery. Glenda was getting down when

"Aagh!" she said and her waters broke. It was now that Hiram finally twigged what was happening. She expected him to panic. Instead he took out the tiny wireless transmitter that Blox had found in one of the Security Guards lockers near to the Arboretum. The tiny in the ear devices; worked like hand units for the Sprites. A bit of modification and they functioned like walkie-talkies. When Gardenia answered instead he was a little shocked

"We know... We both felt her send... it's a wonder you didn't; Blox is getting our transport ready with the things she'll need. Glenda has a place she'll want you to take her; do that fast. We have to leave her there with all she'll need. You know how things go if you know your history. Sprite Females give birth alone" she said. He felt ashamed at all the things he'd said to her

“Oh! Don’t fret. I took it in good humour. I didn’t want you worrying that’s all. My first; and hopefully not the last” she said as he drove the truck as hard as he could to the place Glenda had chosen. The elderly Couple were just arriving in the rear yard and got the message to head for the old Workshops instead. Still invisible… they had had some mischievous fun on the train with the guard and his ticket checks

“We’re not late then” Charlie said

“No she’s late by a few days… I was beginning to worry for her” Whisper said. She and Hamish had got the first Rat expresses they could

“At least nobody will know we’re here. The Security men found nobody ever came near this place; even at night apart from old Fred… he’d set up a sort of still in one part of the building and made his own “shine”. Not to drink… it was far too rough for that. He used it as a metal polish or paint stripper. It worked in either role. It was in a cupboard in the unused part that Glenda had chosen to give birth

“In some respects; I suppose Sprites and Fays are like Cats. Female cats have to find a spot to give birth they like. I remember my Cousin ended up finding a spot under a disused breakdown lorry in a Bus Maintenance garage when she birthed the twins” Halyard said as he and Hermione turned up.
Hamish had remained in the Tower. To keep watch over a new Spark among the Guards. The guy knew his history and was writing a book to be made into a booklet for the Tower Gift shop. To replace an out of date one that was

now well behind the times. That was compiled in the early sixties. The new work and the new Guy were far more accurate and the new Spark had potential to produce a period drama if pushed right. He and Whisper had been working on him alternating every week.

From the sounds in the Cupboard Glenda was having a hard time getting her breathing to work together with the Contractions and the pushes. At one point she cursed loud enough for them to hear outside. And the words were very unpleasant to hear.

“That reminds me of my Aunt Doris the day she caught her Husband sneaking a smoke in the conservatory. Sharp tongued woman that one was” Leona said chuckling. The menfolk tried not to think about what she’d said as it made them all cringe. It was a while before the sound of a new life taking its first breath signified the end of the process; the women went in first. They tidied up Glenda and made the baby; tiny as it was, presentable. She had been very lucky and had not bled. Leona came out and took Charlie to one side

“Leave them wee folk to themselves for now. Hiram has to be in there. I want us to start choosing Girl’s names as we will be asked. Though Hiram is going to be beside himself. The Boy was a quiet one; and has his hair and eyes. By tradition he has to name him” She said

“Girl and boy… twins… Instant family; he’s going to have a rough time of it. At least we might still be around to help. Speaking of which. I wonder what they’ll do for our funerals” Charlie said

“Trust you to put a dampener on things. But still you’re

right in a way. “As a life leaves the world a life comes in to take its place” as my Gran used to say” Leona said

They headed to their old home. They had planned every detail of what they expected. An elderly couple had took an interest; the prediction power to build up enough cash in wins and investments on the stock market etc. to buy their old house and give Sadie and the others a decent legacy. This had been allowed for the Couple to “Die” with relative conviction. Their Wills even stated the profits from the sale should go to them. Leona’s kids got a half share each of her part of the estate. It was all there in black and white. But the sale of the property was the strange bit. It was stated that whatever possessions not bequeathed to the heirs must remain in the property for the use of the buyers. It was a strange request; but as their solicitor had said “Not an unprecedented one. Though it tends to be more common north of the border”. So it was that the Elderly Couple that had bought Sadie’s parents’ house had moved in to a ready furnished place they could be comfortable in. They had enough to keep them for many years. And they could move around later when the time came to end this couple and move on to the next lives. Till they eventually did die that was. Attending their own funerals had been weird though. Sat at the back invisible; then at the Family burial plot… The wake afterwards was perfect. Sadie did them proud. She even baked all the bread herself.

Then the message came that they had to attend the naming ceremony. It was held in a disused boatshed by the Canal. The exterior had been given a coat of special plaster so Graffiti artists could leave their mark and it could be removed when people were fed up with it; for a new group to show their talent. But the interior had simply been cleaned out; painted and left. Nobody understood why; but it just didn't feel right to do anything else with the building. Even the gangs steered clear of it. The Muses used it for meetings and gatherings. Or for special occasions like this one. The babies were very well behaved throughout. Hiram had chosen Victor for the boy. In the end they had all settled on Leona's choice for the girl Symphony. Hamish said it felt right after the power of her lungs had bawled her way into the world. The babies burbled happily in their twins' traveller. It had come from a new range of Doll accessories from the Toy Department. It would be perfect as they grew. To the point they were able to toddle without it. Charlie pulled the men to one side

"You lot gave me a heck of a time trying to figure out what to do about the traditional smoke. I hope these cut Cheroots come close enough to a cigar for you" he said

"Whisper will bawl me oot ah expect. But ye are a man after ma ain heart" Hamish said. The others agreed it was the perfect gesture

"I'll keep this in mind for the next birth" Hiram said. Blox nudged his brother

"Or our event" he said pointing at Gardenia. They all looked a little shocked "Ah; not yet, but we're getting around to it. And she will have plenty of practice looking after the twins when Glenda gets run ragged" he added. And they lit the cheroots and savoured the taste of the fragrant tobacco. Charlie of course had a Cigar. A concession that Leona gave him for this occasion. So long as they stood downwind when smoking them.

“All in all; I think the future is bright… at least I am not the last Muse in the world anymore” Hiram said… the twins gurgled their approval in their own baby talk.

Footnote

People believe in all sorts of things; yet when something they don’t want to believe just happens, they go out of their way to explain it away and then get on with their lives. This propensity of the human race has allowed our Faery Folk siblings to survive our invasion of the world. Long may this be so.
But as for Aliens and such… that’s another story. Just don’t get me started…***don’t!***

Printed in Great Britain
by Amazon